SHERLOCK HOLMES:

REVENANT

William Meikle

Dark Regions Press
–2011–

FIRST TRADE PAPERBACK EDITION

TEXT © 2011 BY WILLIAM MEIKLE

COVER ART © 2011 BY WAYNE MILLER

EDITOR AND PUBLISHER, JOE MOREY

ISBN: 978-1-937128-24-1

COVER AND INTERIOR DESIGN BY
STEPHEN JAMES PRICE
WWW.BOOKLOOKSDESIGN.COM

DARK REGIONS PRESS
PO BOX 1264
COLUSA, CA 95932
WWW.DARKREGIONS.COM

Grateful acknowledgment to Conan Doyle Estate Ltd. for permission to use the Sherlock Holmes Characters created by the late Sir Arthur Conan Doyle.

Dedication

To Baker Street Irregulars everywhere.

Chapter One

Holmes has often berated me for a perceived habit of sensationalizing his cases in the writing down of the details. But in this particular matter there is so much that is already sensational that I fear I may under-report the import of them.

It began in September. I was late. The lecture in the Royal Hospital overran by some thirty minutes... thirty minutes of the driest of exposition on potential cures for tropical diseases. Things did not improve when I emerged into a rainstorm that meant all carriages were already taken. I had a choice to either stay in shelter or brave the elements. I did not have my heavy overcoat with me so I decided to wait the rain out. It proved a bad decision as it continued for almost an hour in a steady downpour.

It was already mid-morning by the time I arrived back in Baker Street and, knowing that Holmes would be getting impatient, I was in no mood for any further delay.

I say this in mitigation of my next actions. If I had paid more heed for those next few seconds much grief may have been averted later. But at the time I was more than a little annoyed to have a derelict stand in my path as I got down out of the carriage.

I took him for one of the itinerant beggars who have so recently plagued the area. In my heart I knew that many of them were in the situation of having to beg to eat through no fault of their own, but the man with the twisted lip had put me permanently on guard against blaggards and con men. I might have given him a penny just to get rid of him but I was already making excuses to Holmes in my mind. The vagrant stood directly in my path, and when I made to dodge around him he moved to block me.

"Move aside please," I said, trying to control a rising irritation. He did not give way. He was small, with a stoop that bent his head into deep shadow under a wide-brimmed hat. Wisps of straggly red hair showed under the brim. His clothes were of heavy cheap cotton, threadbare and muddy from head to toe, and his feet were bare showing cracked and split nails also caked in fresh mud.

"Can I help you?" I said, expecting him to put out a begging hand. Instead he seemed to ignore me. He muttered to himself, rapidly, a repeating pattern as if reciting his multiplication tables. It also sounded like something was *broken* inside his chest – a rumble that spoke of deep-seated bronchitis or some similar ailment.

And that is as much as I remembered of him later, beyond the fact that when he finally spoke to me he had a broad Scots accent. And the words he spoke took me aback so much that I completely forgot to reply.

"Mr. Holmes will have need of this before the week is out," he said, and passed me a sheet of paper. I took it, and looked up to see him walking rapidly away in the kind of skipping gait you sometimes see in men who have suffered a badly set break in one leg. I might have followed him were I not already acutely aware of just how late I was for my appointment with Holmes.

I was, however, just curious enough to check what I

had been given. The sheet of paper did not enlighten me any. It had been torn roughly from a book, and was an illuminated diagram titled *MALAGMA*. It showed a fiery red serpent eating the world, depicted as a shining golden disc hanging above an ocean. The page was also getting rather wet as more rain started to fall, heavy spatters of it threatening to turn the paper to a soggy mush. I folded it in half and put it in my inner pocket as I entered 221B Baker Street.

Holmes stood in the hallway waiting for me. I don't know how long he'd been there, but it had been more than long enough to make him irritable – that was immediately obvious. I have seen Sherlock Holmes in many moods over the years of our acquaintance, but I do believe that this was also the only time he appeared to be flustered.

"You have been tardy Watson," he said, turning me around in the hall before I could even remove my hat. He passed me my heavy overcoat and almost marched me back outside while I struggled with the garment. "I would have gone without you had they not specifically requested that you join me."

"They?"

I did not get an answer. Instead I was shepherded onto the pavement. As we approached the kerb Holmes hailed a carriage and one stopped for him immediately. I did not hear his instructions to the driver as I was bundled quickly inside, but they must have been insistent for we set off at a rapid trot across the cobbles.

Holmes would not be drawn as to our destination; indeed he sat quiet for the whole journey, lost either in concentration or irritation, I knew not which. Given the manner in which I had been greeted, I more than expected it to be irritation.

I gathered we were about to embark on a new case.

SHERLOCK HOLMES: REVENANT

That thought gave me some satisfaction, for my friend had been moody of late due to a lack of activity to fuel his ever-busy mind. I had recently suffered several nights of his black gloom, attempting conversation only to be met with a taciturn sullen silence. If there was work ahead, I hoped it would be enough to lift him out of it, for a time at least.

The carriage took us south to Piccadilly Circus and then towards the river, which annoyed me somewhat for if Holmes had intimated our destination to me in advance I could have met him much earlier without having to return to Baker Street. But when I mentioned this fact all I got in reply was an irritated grunt. In truth I was glad when the journey came to an end, for Holmes in a temper is a most disagreeable travelling companion.

Much to my surprise we were deposited outside the Houses of Parliament. Flanked by two sullen policemen we were led at a march to the Member's Lounge for the Lords. Whatever matter had aroused Holmes into his present state of irritation, it seemed it was an important one.

The police left us at the door. Three people waited inside for us in an otherwise empty Member's Lounge – two standing in animated discussion and the other slumped unmoving in an armchair. The taller of the two standing men turned and I recognized his bulky figure immediately. It was only then that Holmes spoke.

"I do hope this is not another of your cast-off cases Mycroft? You know that my preferred choice of adversary is always the criminal rather than the politician, despite the fact that there is often little to tell them apart."

For my part I now knew exactly what had irritated my friend so. To be *summoned* by his elder brother must have vexed Holmes severely, but he had been so lacking in work for that great brain of his that he would endure it for the chance of a fresh case. That did not, however, mean that he had to like it, nor that he had to hide his irritability.

Mycroft paid his brother no heed. He dismissed the man he had been speaking to with a curt wave of the hand. It was only when the three of us were alone with the man in the chair that Mycroft turned to me.

"I need your medical opinion Doctor Watson," he said. "As you can see, Lord Menzies here is somewhat indisposed."

I did not for one minute believe that I had been brought to the Lords for my *medical opinion*. There was a perfectly good infirmary in the building itself, staffed by a reliable man I knew well from my army days. No, this was part of the game that was always playing between the brothers; I just happened to be caught in the middle, and not for the first time. There was however an obviously sick man who needed attention, so I decided I would attend to him and leave the brothers to their own devices.

"Watson?" Mycroft said, and I was surprised to hear some irritability there, a rare thing from a man with a normally languid disposition. He motioned with a tilt of his head toward the slumped figure and I gave in to the inevitable.

My patient was an elderly gentleman, well dressed but somewhat rumpled, with what looked like an egg stain on the left lapel of his waistcoat and several streaks of ash on the other side that had been rubbed in rather than brushed away. His hair had that oily sheen you see in vain men of a certain age, and was so thin as to show liver spots on his scalp.

When I bent to examine him I spotted several other

things almost immediately. He was most definitely alive. He breathed deeply and regularly and had the calm pulse of someone who was fast asleep. He was completely unconscious despite having his eyes wide open. His pupils did not respond to direct light, nor was there any reaction when I snapped my fingers by his ears. I folded one of his legs over the other, with some difficulty as there seemed to be no *give* there, almost as if rigor was setting in. He did however show a reflex when I struck just below his knee. He also seemed to be attempting to speak in so far as his lips moved, but no sounds were forthcoming. His hands felt somewhat cold and clammy to the touch, but there was no obvious sign of any kind of violence having been done on his person. I checked his head, searching under the hair for bumps or bruising but there was no sign of trauma.

I must admit I was completely stumped. I could only surmise a condition of the brain, although it was one I had never previously encountered.

"Well Watson, what is your diagnosis?" Mycroft said. He still had not acknowledged Holmes but I was now far too concerned for the stricken man to bother myself with fraternal politics.

"He has taken some kind of seizure by the looks of things," I said as I stood back. "This man needs to be removed to a hospital as soon as can be. There may be a buildup of fluid in the brain causing these symptoms. Any delay in getting him the proper treatment could prove fatal."

I looked around in search of some support. None was forthcoming. Mycroft shook his head and did not seem in the least bit perturbed.

"I'm afraid that will not be possible Doctor. Let us sit a while," he said. "We shall wait and see what occurs next."

"Why ask that I bring Watson at all if you are merely going to ignore his counsel?" Holmes said, giving voice to the same question I was asking myself.

Mycroft however was most insistent.

"I did not bring you here merely to see a sick man," he said. "There is more to this than meets the eye, and I can assure you that your trip has not been in vain. Now please, sit. This should not take long."

I could see that Holmes was on the point of becoming agitated, and I too was loath to remain quiet while a sick man suffered in front of me. However Mycroft seemed to be taking it most calmly, so much so that he went to the door at the far end of the room and called for drinks to be brought from the bar. Holmes finally relented and, following his lead, I sat opposite the stricken man and lit a pipe. I did however watch the man most carefully, determined to act at any change in his condition.

There followed a strained ten minutes where we all tried not to stare at the slumped figure in the chair. Mycroft seemed completely unconcerned about the poor man's predicament and indeed launched into a lengthy anecdote about some drunken shenanigans that had taken place in this very room some three nights previously. I feigned attention but Holmes' mind was elsewhere. He spent several minutes in closely studying the Lord's mouth as it opened and closed but if he was able to make any sense from the lip-reading he said nothing.

After a time I could take it no more.

"Dash it all Mycroft, I may be a bally bad doctor, but I took an oath, and that oath will not allow me to remain quiet a minute longer. The poor chap's mind may be leaving him even while we sit here. I will not tolerate it."

Still Mycroft did not flinch. And much to my surprise Holmes took his brother's side in the matter.

"I know it vexes you Watson but please, just a few minutes longer? Mycroft, for all his faults, never does anything without good reason."

By this time Holmes himself had risen from his seat and had started pacing the floor. I could see that he would not nay-say Mycroft's wishes in his older brother's domain. I was about to make my case in a more forcible manner when the most remarkable thing happened.

Lord Menzies sat up straight, shook himself like a dog shedding water and inquired whether he might not 'Have a little port and brandy if that would be all right?'

I was up and at his side in a flash, pushing him back in his chair when he showed signs of wanting to rise.

"Please, sit still," I said. "I'm a doctor."

"A doctor?" he said, his voice full of outrage. "Why in blazes would I need a bally doctor? I am as fit as a butcher's dog."

And much to my astonishment it seemed he was. His breathing and pulse were as measured as before, but now he was in complete possession of all his faculties.

"I say old chap," the Lord said as I snapped my fingers at his ears. "Steady on there. You could do me a mischief."

There was no sign that only seconds before this man had been unconscious and unresponsive. I did not know what to make of it and the Lord himself was of no help. He became agitated at being the focus of so much attention.

"I say lads, play the game. Tell me what's going on here."

"We were rather hoping you could tell us?" Mycroft said.

"Fell asleep in the bally armchair is what happened. Too much kedgeree for breakfast I should think."

Holmes had still not spoken up but I could see he was less agitated now and clearly interested in the proceedings. My admiration for Mycroft went up a notch. He knew exactly how to ensnare Holmes' interest; not by telling him what was going on, but by letting him see for himself.

At that moment Lord Menzies stood without a hint of unsteadiness and bade us a good day.

"You should take it easy for the rest of the day my Lord," I said. "You have had a bit of a turn."

He looked at me as if he suspected I was making fun of him.

"A turn? I don't know what they teach doctors these days, but I have never felt better."

And with that he left us for the comforts of the bar. Holmes and I allowed Mycroft to take us to a quiet corner of the room and, over a smoke and a drink, he finally explained to us why we had been brought here.

"It will be obvious to you by now that I did not ask you here on a whim. This is the fifth such occurrence in the past month," he said. "And all have ended the same way, with the Lord in question having no knowledge of anything untoward having happened." He went on to give us more details of each case, but really there was little more to tell. We had a genuine mystery on our hands, and Holmes had a new case.

««—»»»

Holmes did not speak to me until we were in a carriage.

"Well Watson, what do you make of it?"

I mentally reviewed what Mycroft had told us before replying.

"It does seem that there is too much of a pattern to it

for it to be coincidence," I replied. "Five prominent politicians, all struck with the same malady in such close succession, and all recovered with no memory of anything untoward. It is dashed peculiar, and I can see why Mycroft would be worried. Such a thing could easily become a matter of national security in short order."

Holmes nodded in agreement.

"Dashed peculiar indeed. But I fear there is someone at work here with a deeper purpose in mind. Mark my words Watson, this case will have depths as yet unplumbed. Mycroft smells a rat; that is why he has asked for my involvement. He may well be the most lazy man in the Empire, but his instincts in matters such as this are sound."

This second carriage trip proved much more congenial than the first, and Holmes even managed a smile at several points. The mere fact of having work for his mind seemed somehow to energize him, bringing forward the part of him that was most vibrant, the part of him that actually enjoyed life. I called him my friend in whatever mood he chose to show the world, but *this* was the way I preferred to see him.

We started work on the case immediately. Before we left Parliament Mycroft had arranged for us to have access to the London residence of Lord Menzies. The carriage dropped us off in Belgravia outside a tall mid-terraced block of the most handsome dwellings and we were shown inside by a butler who insisted on following us around as if fearful we might abscond with the family silver.

He need not have worried. Lord Menzies obviously preferred a Spartan life-style and there was little in his lodgings to show for his presence beyond an obvious pride in his homeland; there were large portraits of his ancestors in full regalia, and a family crest done in the finest needlework on a large hanging tapestry.

"Tell me," Holmes asked the butler as we stood over a desk in what was clearly a study. "Was there anything strange in his Lordship's manner in recent days?"

The butler, clearly staunchly loyal to his charge, was slow to reply. I thought Holmes might offer a bribe, then realized that would be the wrong move with this man. All that an offer of money would get us would be hurt pride and outrage. Holmes as usual was ahead of me, using honey instead of vinegar.

"Anything you tell us will of course be kept in the strictest of confidence," he said. "My friend here is a doctor and he is most concerned about his Lordship's welfare."

The butler visibly softened at that, and took me into his confidence in the way that people often will with a medical man when they will talk to no one else.

"It was last Saturday," he began. "A cold night if you remember? I was downstairs stoking the fire when I heard a *thud*, as if a body had fallen to the floor upstairs. I immediately went to investigate for, as you know, his Lordship is not a young man. But just as I got to the door a voice called out, saying that everything was all right. It sounded a bit odd, like his Lordship, but then again, not really like him at all. But he called out my name and bid me enter. I stood, by this desk here, while he wrote two letters. After that, despite the lateness of the hour, he had me deliver them, saying they were *most urgent matters of state.*

"He still sounded strange to me, more English than Scottish. I know I am not explaining this very well, for it was obviously my Lord sitting in the chair at the desk. But it did not *feel* like him.

"I did as I was asked and delivered the letters. But

the funny thing is, in the morning he did not mention them again and did not ask whether they had been successfully dispatched. That again was most unlike the man, although by then he was at least back to speaking in his normal accent."

The butler suddenly seemed to realize that he was giving away perhaps *too* much of his Lordship's confidences and went quiet. He would only answer one last question from Holmes.

"Did you perchance see to whom these letters were addressed?"

"Only the top one of the two," the butler said. "And I remember it because it obviously *was* a matter of some import, for it was addressed to no less than the Home Secretary."

After that encounter Holmes had little more than a perfunctory stroll round the rest of the house, then led me back out onto the pavement.

"We will find nothing more here Watson," he said. "The key to this case lies in the positions of the men themselves. That, and their shared background."

"Shared?"

"Why yes," Holmes said. "Mycroft did not explicitly mention it, but I know enough of the peerage to say with some certainty that the afflicted men can all claim Scots heritage. I am sure we will find when we check that all five of them have a family history in that land going back for many centuries."

Holmes hailed a carriage to take us back to Baker Street. When one pulled up and we entered I reached for my cheroot case and my fingers touched the piece of paper the vagrant had forced on me. I had completely forgotten my earlier encounter.

"Speaking of Scotsmen," I said, taking out the page and handing it to Holmes. "What do you make of this?"

I told Holmes the details of my meeting in the street earlier that morning. He listened attentively, not unfolding the page until after I was finished.

"My dear Watson," he said. "I do not believe in coincidences. You must endeavor to pay more attention in future. You never know when something might have a bearing on a case."

He spent some time studying the page. He rubbed the sheet between his fingers.

"Late Elizabethan text," he said. "Possibly in itself Scottish. The ink has that peculiar red tint often seen in manuscripts of this age from north of the border. The paper seems authentic for the same period; late Sixteenth or early Seventeenth century at a guess, and probably from Spielman's mill in Dartford judging by the texture and flocking."

He paused as if in thought then started to quote.

In open show, then Sundry secret toys
Make rotten rags to yield a thickened froth
There it is stamped and washed as white as snow
Then flung on frame and hanged to dry, I trow
Thus paper straight it is to write upon
As it were rubbed and smoothed with slicking stone

Holmes smiled. "A piece of doggerel from the time... by Thomas Churchyard I believe."

To me it was just another astonishing example of Holmes' capacity to memorize even the most obscure of things, laying them away against a later time when they might prove useful.

"And of course the symbol in the drawing is alchemical in nature," he continued.

"What do you mean, alchemical?"

"If you ask a lay person, they will tell you it means

the search for the method of turning lead into gold but, as anyone who has delved onto the mysteries knows, that is just a metaphor. No, the *great quest* is the search for illumination through the perfection of body and spirit."

He traced a finger round the drawing of the serpent.

"Strictly speaking," he said. "This drawing does not represent part of the process at all, rather, this is a symbolic representation of the whole. *Malagma* is Latin, meaning *Amalgamation*. The whole process, the great quest if you like, is to amalgamate the soul, the *microcosm*, with the universe, the *macrocosm*."

"Sorry," I said, trying a smile. "You've lost me old man."

Holmes laughed.

"I thought I might. Alchemical symbolism was obscure even back when it was a relatively common practice among scientists and mystics alike. Let us just say the serpent represents the totality of existence, and the circle inside is the bounds of our mortal life. The goal of alchemy is to break the boundary – to gain access to the greater circle beyond. For some that is thought to mean eternal life, for others it is a quest for enlightenment and a chance of a glimpse at the inner workings of the universe. In either case," he said, waving the paper at me. "*This* is a clue. I told you this case had hidden depths. We are headed into murky waters, Watson. Very murky indeed."

He handed the page back to me.

"Hold onto this old man. And if you receive any others like it, be sure to tell me in a more timely manner." He smiled to let me know it was not a rebuke, and we lit up smokes. On the way back to Baker Street he pondered aloud about the mystery at hand.

"There is most definitely a pattern of sorts here

Watson," he said. "One that we must discern if we are to pierce the veils that hide it from us. We must ask ourselves several questions." He ticked them off on his fingers. "Firstly, why have these men in particular been targeted? Secondly, why now? And lastly... what is the overall purpose behind these attacks? For, be sure of that one thing if nothing else, there is most definitely a purpose. I will stake my reputation on it."

««(—)»»

Once back in the apartment in Baker Street Holmes wasted no time.

"Have Mrs. Hudson fetch some lunch," he said. "I have a book here on the genealogy of the peers of Scotland that I must track down. I have not seen it for some time."

I believe I have mentioned in my notes on previous cases that Holmes' filing methods left something to be desired, being a system peculiar to Holmes himself and one that only he knew the secret of unlocking. To the rest of us it looked less like a system and more like a haphazard jumble of papers, books and journals all piled in stacks of various heights in corners and against the walls of the apartment.

But as usual Holmes was able to find what he was looking for when anyone else would have thrown their hands up in defeat. By the time I returned from making my request to Mrs. Hudson he had a book in his hand.

"My guess has proved right," he said. "All five men did indeed have Scots heritage going back several centuries at least, with numerous shared ancestors; not surprising given the closed nature of the aristocracy in that small country over the centuries. We must find out how long ago any connection might be. The solution to our mystery may indeed lie far back in history."

SHERLOCK HOLMES: REVENANT

Holmes started pulling more books from shelves in his small library, and I knew from experience that he now had the bit firmly between his teeth. It looked like the search would take him some time so I sat at the desk in the corner and made some notes while the events of the day were still fresh in my mind.

Not long afterwards Mrs. Hudson arrived with a tray of pies and cold meat sandwiches which she bullied Holmes into eating, but, as ever when a case took hold, food ceased to be a pleasure for him and became little more than fuel to keep him awake and thinking. He shovelled some bread down quickly then went straight back to his hunt. I treated myself to a more leisurely lunch and can report that the pork pies Mrs. Hudson provided were among the best I had ever tasted.

Over the next hour Holmes asked me two questions, both regarding the dates on which Mycroft had indicated the attacks had occurred. Apart from that he seemed lost in study of a series of older leather-bound books. After a while he took himself off to the fireside chair and lit his favourite pipe while scribbling a series of notes on a pad.

It was late afternoon before he spoke again.

"I think I have something Watson, but it may well involve an all-night vigil. Are you up for it?"

"You know me old chap, always willing to help."

"Good man. But first I had better explain my thinking. You will remember the five *attacks* on their Lordships? Plotting the time frame was most illuminating. There is a definite pattern, and one I am sure Mycroft has already ascertained. There were sixteen days between the first and second attacks, eight between the second and third, four until the fourth and just two before the very scenes we witnessed today in the Lords. If I am right, and I am sure that I am, the next attack will be sometime in the following twenty hours. And I believe I have narrowed down the possible victims to two men only."

At that he left me alone in the room for a spell, and I heard him dictate a telegram to Mrs. Hudson. I did not catch the full gist of it but it appeared to be instructions for Mycroft to arrange that the intended *victims* be brought together and put under protection until Holmes and I could get there.

"Best got your ablutions done now old chap," he said on his return. "As I have already intimated, we may have a long night ahead of us."

I felt the old excitement rise as I made my toilet. I had realized long ago that one of the reasons I chose to help Holmes in his cases was an urge to feel that same excitement I had felt in my military service, the quickening of the senses that told me I was fully alive. Holmes was not the only one who needed a case.

After a quick wash and shave I found Holmes already dressed and waiting by the apartment door, eager for our departure and the chance of some action.

"Hurry man," he said. "It would not do for a doctor to be late twice in one day. People might think it to be a habit."

It was only once we were in a carriage and heading for Parliament that he allowed me fully into his thinking.

"You may have noticed my perusal of the genealogy books earlier," he said. "I thought there might be an answer in there, a connection as yet unnoticed. And indeed my reading threw up one most pertinent fact. The five victims so far have all shared a common ancestor in a minor Scottish Earl in the Sixteenth Century. After that initial finding it did not take me too much longer to ascertain that there are only two other members of the House with this same characteristic; Lord Crawford of Cunninghame and Lord Douglas of Dunottar. And as luck would have it both are currently in town. By the time we arrive at our destination Mycroft will have ensured that they will be in Parliament to meet us."

"And then what?" I asked. "I don't know that there is any *medical* solution should one or the other of them be afflicted like the rest, and I cannot for the life of me think of any course of action we might take to prevent it happening."

Holmes pursed his lips.

"We shall see what we shall see. I doubt that we are near the end of the matter, but we may be near the end of the beginning. If I am there when the attack happens I may spot something that has as yet remained hidden. Vigilance Watson. That is what is required now."

«««—»»»

On arrival back at Parliament we were immediately shown up a steep flight of steps beside the chamber of the House of Lords; an area of the great building I had never before visited. It was all marble flooring and oak panelling with impressive landscape paintings at regular intervals. Our footsteps echoed sharply as we walked down a long empty corridor. Mycroft was nowhere to be seen but a young policeman showed us to the rooms where the two Lords were waiting for the night's vigil.

"I had them put in separate rooms," Holmes said. "I thought it best to keep them apart. We shall take one Lord each, watch them closely, and see what we shall see. You take Crawford, and I'll take Douglas. I'll be just down the hall, so call out if you need assistance. Keep an eye open for anything that seems untoward, and record all that happens. It may be that there will only be another bout of unconsciousness to deal with, but we must be prepared for any eventuality."

At that Holmes went off along the corridor, leaving me beside a young constable who looked nervous as he opened the door and showed me inside. I was immediately faced with a slightly irate Scottish Lord. He was red in the cheeks and around the nose and at the time I was unsure whether that was due to his temper or his drinking habits.

"This won't do you know?" Crawford said as I entered the room. "It won't do at all. What is so damned important that it will keep me from my bed tonight?"

He turned towards me and looked me up and down.

"Doctor Watson?"

I nodded, walked over to him and shook his hand.

"I don't suppose you have anything you can tell me about this dashed nuisance?" he asked.

"Apart from the fact that there seems to be no immediate danger to you other than falling asleep in the chair, no."

That only irritated him further.

"On top of missing my bed later, I am supposed to be in the chamber this evening, speaking in a debate on reforming the House."

"It wouldn't do to fall asleep there," I said, and got a laugh from him.

"With some of the members it would be hard to tell the difference."

He laughed again, and finally he seemed to relax somewhat. "Tell me, are you a whisky or a brandy man?" he asked. He moved over to a cabinet against the wall and opened the door to reveal an array of liquor bottles.

"I need to keep my wits about me," I said. "Lest

anything happens to you."

"Stuff and nonsense," Crawford said. "Old Menzies told me you made a fuss over him falling asleep this morning. I know, for a fact, the old man has whisky for breakfast, lunch and dinner. 'Tis no wonder he was sleeping in the members' lounge. The wonder is he isn't caught out more often. Now, have a drink with me man. I refuse to drink alone for that way lies ruin." His accent showed more strongly every minute as he fell into a more conversational tone of voice. "Many a good man has been brought low through solitary drinking. But I'll be damned if I will sit here all night waiting for the Lord knows what calumny without a drink in my hand."

I settled for a small Scotch then spent the next hour watching the man consume the larger part of a bottle on his own. I will say this for him; he handled it better than I would have done. He also had some excellent pipe tobacco and we soon had a fug swirling around the fireplace.

I needn't have worried about how we would pass the time as he proved to be an excellent conversationalist. He was at pains to avoid *'shop talk'*, instead choosing mostly to remark on sporting matters. We found a common point of interest in the game of rugger and the university teams in particular. He had strong opinions on the way the game should be played that diverged wildly from current coaching standards. I found myself in agreement with much that he said, and became so engrossed in the discussion that the next hour passed most agreeably before the alcohol started to take its effect on him. I was just relating my tale of a match we had arranged in the palace of the Maharajah when I spotted that his Lordship had fallen asleep, the Scotch having finally taken hold. I almost laughed when I realized that he was already almost exactly in the same state I had been told to be alert for. If it had not been for the fact that his eyes were closed and that he started to snore softly I might not have been able to tell the difference.

So began a long lonely evening. At first I was content to spend my time staring into space and smoking my pipe, but as night came and the old building fell quiet I started to get the jitters and prowled the room looking for something to keep my mind busy. The books on the shelves were little help, being mostly dusty tomes concerning laws and binders of regulations and paperwork, many of them to do with building works currently underway in the city.

His Lordship had a large fine mahogany desk and I thought I might find some less dry reading material there, but the desk was neat, tidy, and bare of anything except an inkstand and a blotter. Just as I was despairing, I found a pack of cards tucked in a corner of one of the bookcases. I was able to pass the time on games of solitaire, all the while accompanied by his Lordship's soft snoring and the tolling of the tower bell to mark the passage of the hours.

At some point after nine o'clock I rose to stretch my legs. I lit a pipe and went to the window but all I could see was my own reflection and beyond that only a handful of lights showing on the south side of the Thames. I turned back to the room.

And that is when it happened. The first indication I had that something was amiss was when his Lordship finally stopped snoring. I thought it might be a sign that he was about to come up out of his whisky-induced stupor, but he was perfectly still. I bent to check on him. He had that same blank stare and regular breathing I had noted in Lord Menzies the morning before. And once again the victim's mouth moved, although no words came. As I had done earlier I made a thorough examination. It seemed that his Lordship had been struck by the same affliction as his countryman Menzies.

I was about to notify Holmes of the situation when Crawford's head came up. The eyes that looked up at me were clear with no sign of any effect of whisky there. He smiled broadly and spoke, in clipped English tones totally at odds with the soft Scots accent he had sported earlier.

"Well, well, if it isn't the faithful dog? If you are here, that must mean Holmes is with the other one?"

I was so taken aback by the change in the man that I did not reply. As quickly as it had started the smile faded. Crawford's head fell forward, he slumped slightly in his seat and several seconds later he started to snore again.

Less than a minute later I heard a loud crash of breaking glass from somewhere close by. I ran out into the corridor and dashed past the young police officer. He seemed startled and unsure as to what to do.

"Holmes?" I called and was mightily relieved when he answered.

"In here Watson."

I entered the office and found Holmes standing alone in the room, white faced, staring out from a broken window to the terrace some thirty feet below. I went over next to him and peered out carefully. A body lay broken on the flagstones with blood, showing black in the gaslight, already pooling around his head. The man was obviously dead. As I looked two policemen approached the body. They looked up to see Holmes and I staring down at them. Holmes pulled me back inside.

"It's a rum do Watson. He jumped and I could do nothing to stop him. We were discussing the situation in the Sudan when he twitched, stood, smiled at me and leapt for the window. It all happened in less than five seconds."

I had no time to ask for more details, for things happened very quickly after that.

"What *have* you done?" a clipped English voice said behind me. I turned to see Lord Crawford standing in the doorway, showing no sign of any malady. The young policeman stood at his shoulder.

"Arrest these men," Crawford said. "They have murdered Lord Douglas."

It took several seconds for me to realize that he meant Holmes and I, and even then I was of a mind to stand and argue our case, but Holmes had other ideas.

"The trap is sprung Watson, and we are caught. Follow me."

He passed me at a run, knocking Lord Crawford and the young policeman to one side. I hesitated only for a second, just long enough to see Crawford smile as he picked himself up from the floor, then I followed my friend. The sound of a police whistle echoed along the corridor behind us.

«««—»»»

So it was that we became fugitives from justice.

My mind was a whirl of images; of Crawford staring at me, bright eyed despite the whisky, of Holmes standing at the smashed and broken window, and of the poor broken body of Lord Douglas, blood seeping on the flagstones. I had no time to try to make sense of it then, being too busy with our attempt to flee.

The first part of the night passed in such a blur that I scarce remember half of it now. I followed behind Holmes as we ran down the long empty corridor, having some difficulty keeping up with his obvious haste. At the far end of the corridor a policeman arrived at the top of the stairs and stood with a hand up, blocking our way.

"Halt!" he shouted.

Holmes kept running and with seemingly no compunction at all, knocked the policeman aside with a blow to the head that sent the man reeling. In other circumstances I may have stopped to check on the prone figure to ensure there was no sign of concussion but Holmes would have none of it.

"Hurry man. I was not joking about the trap being sprung. I have no doubt that preparations had already been made for our apprehension before we even got here. So let there be no dawdling. For tonight at least, forget that you are a doctor."

And with that he sped off down the long staircase. I was still of a mind to stay and explain myself, but I have trusted Holmes' judgement all these years; far too much to go against his will at such a time, even if it might mean complete ruin to follow his lead. I went after him, already limping slightly with the effort but determined to keep up.

Quite how we managed to escape from the Parliament building itself without being apprehended is something of a mystery to me. Holmes said later that he believed Mycroft may have had a hand in ensuring that the policemen on duty were looking elsewhere at the opportune moment, but whatever the case we ran through the main entrance hall without being stopped. With a curt waved good-bye to a startled watchman we were soon out into the night air of Westminster. Almost immediately more police whistles came from all around us but Holmes seemed calmer now that we had escaped from the building itself.

"The battle can now be fought on more equitable

terms," he said. "We have wrested away his territorial advantage. Now we must make the most of it."

I was still unsure whom Holmes might be referring to, but he gave me no time to reply. He led me along the north embankment for several hundred yards then, as another shrill whistle and the first heavy footsteps of pursuit sounded behind us took a sharp turn up into the warren of back streets around Charing Cross railway station. More whistles were raised in pursuit but Holmes seemed unconcerned. He took us through the front door of a busy public bar and out again through the kitchen at the rear, oblivious to the complaints of the staff. That brought us out into a tall narrow alleyway that I never even knew existed, but with which Holmes seemed completely familiar.

"Come Watson. We should be clear soon," he said.

Without slowing down we headed north again and quickly emerged into the Strand where we mingled with the theatre crowds before turning up towards Covent Garden. There was now a rising tumult of police activity, but it was all some way away in the distance and by the time we left Long Acre behind there was no sign of any pursuit whatsoever.

It seemed we had indeed got clear away. For the present at least.

We slowed to a brisk walk and started our way north towards Tottenham Court Road. I turned to look behind us, then again a few yards later when I heard a whistle. Holmes put a hand on my shoulder.

"Gently now Watson," Holmes said. "I think we have drawn quite enough attention to ourselves for one night. Let us pretend we are two gentlemen strolling home from the theatre."

We certainly were not out of place here close to the center; numerous groups of people were out on what was a fine dry night after the earlier rain, and we were able to continue for a while without any notice being taken of us. But once north of the junction with Oxford Street the crowds thinned out somewhat and we needed to be more circumspect.

I thought Holmes intended to make for Baker Street but instead of going to the left we turned right at the top of the road and made for the King's Cross area.

"The Yard will be on our heels again soon enough Watson," he said as he strode, moving faster again, almost at a run. "We cannot give them any easy opportunities to trap us. I will not be tricked twice in one night. We must become invisible before we can proceed."

"How will that be possible Holmes? You are one of the most recognized men in London."

He did not reply, but I soon found out his intention. He led me round the east side of King's Cross station then up and over a rather tall brick wall that required him to give me a hand up before I could clamber over to join him. After checking that we had not been seen he strode across several sets of tracks, past some badly rusted trailer beds and bogeys to what I took to be an empty cargo container. It too was in a state of some disrepair, being badly corroded and weather-beaten, but the main sliding door seemed solid enough. It was held closed by a shiny, almost new, lock. To my amazement Holmes opened it with a key from his fob, slid the door open, and boosted me up inside.

"Welcome to my bolt-hole," he said. He clambered up to join me and pulled the door closed, leaving us in pitch darkness.

"Don't move Watson," he said. "I'll get us some light." I heard the scrape of a match and saw the flare in the dark as Holmes lit a candle. The smoke from the wick wafted in the still air and my gaze followed it up to where it escaped through a small vent in the ceiling. There was now enough light to make out that Holmes' *bolt-hole* was rather well appointed; there were several sturdy armoires filled with clothes, a desk with a large mirror below which the accoutrements of Holmes' various disguises lay scattered, and even a single armchair sitting beside a tall well-stocked bookcase.

Holmes laughed at my obvious confusion.

"I keep this place for those cases when I do not have time to make a return to Baker Street. I got the idea from Neville St. Clair. Remember how he had a secret place where he could change character completely? I have found it useful several times in the past, but surely none more so than tonight. Only a few people know of its presence, and I trust them all to keep that knowledge private."

"I do hope one of the others isn't Lestrade?" I said, and that got me another laugh.

"No Watson, you can have no fears on that score. But it is Inspector Lestrade we must consider now. We need to get out of London, and quickly. Unfortunately Scotland Yard knows my methods and will be watching all of the more obvious escape routes."

"Leave London? But surely we must stay? Stay and clear our names?"

"It is clearing our names that requires us to leave," Holmes said. "We must go to Scotland, and with some haste. Someone has gone to a great deal of trouble to embroil us in this matter. That amount of effort means that the ultimate goal must be a matter of some import. I am worried Watson, worried that we have already been outflanked before we have properly begun."

"But why Scotland?"

"The answer lies in the bloodlines of the men

involved, of that I am certain. We must follow that line of enquiry. But we shall have to be cautious; for our adversary will also know that we will be on his trail."

Holmes started to pull clothes from the armoires.

"We must travel incognito Watson. Which would you prefer?" He held up a heavy overcoat in one hand. "A sailor making his way home from the North Atlantic run? Or maybe an itinerant laborer looking for work?"

"You seem to be taking the night's events very calmly old man," I said.

Holmes had already moved over to the mirror and started applying make-up to make his face look darker and more unwashed.

"On the contrary Watson," he replied. "This is a matter of the utmost import. I must contact Mycroft at the earliest opportunity and have him watch Lord Douglas closely – although I have no doubt that he will already have that matter in hand. But our priority for tonight is to get out of the city unnoticed. And for that, we need a disguise."

I finally relented and spent a most uncomfortable ten minutes allowing Holmes to apply some rather noxious stage make-up to my hands and face. After that he had me choose some clothing for my *disguise* which thankfully proved cleaner and less smelly than it looked to be. Lastly he made me ditch my pipe, my cigarette case and my lighter.

"All would betray us immediately to a trained eye I'm afraid," he said. "But they will be safe here until our return. And fear not, we shall not be short of smoking materials." He handed me a threadbare tobacco pouch and some rather rough papers. "An old soldier like you can surely roll his own given the makings?"

I was immediately hit with a memory of a cold clear night in the hills of Afghanistan, drinking gin and listening to the sound of drums in the wind while smoking a succession of thin cigarettes and waiting for dawn... when the fighting would start. Sitting there in that converted railway carriage, I was a long way from those hills. But the feeling of tense apprehension was almost exactly the same in both cases. I pushed it down. I had learned long ago that what was to come would come in its own sweet time, and worrying about it rarely changed the outcome in the slightest. I concentrated on trying to make my disguise as convincing as possible.

Minutes later we both stood in front of the mirror surveying our new personas. We certainly looked like the pair of itinerant laborers that Holmes intended us to be, and I started to hope that we might succeed in our plan of evading capture. Holmes also showed me the pocket in his belt into which he had sewn a pouch containing five-pound notes and gold guineas. "Just so any fear of us starving on the journey you may have is allayed."

And with that we went once more into the night, our only luggage a battered Gladstone bag containing some fresh clothing and a pair of revolvers hidden in a false bottom.

«««—»»»

Our escape was almost foiled before it had properly begun.

"I think the disguises will stand up to scrutiny," Holmes said. "What say we try for a train? It will be risky, but the alternative is to start walking, and it is a long way to Scotland."

I agreed readily enough, for my old wound was already stiff and sore after the walk from Westminster, and the thought of more exertion so soon afterwards did

SHERLOCK HOLMES: REVENANT

not appeal in the slightest. I was not however completely at ease in disguise, not having either Holmes' aptitude or experience in pretending to be someone other than myself. I felt self-conscious as I walked by his side, taking a long circuitous route around the outskirts of the station to arrive back at the main entrance some thirty minutes later.

I only started to relax somewhat when we split up and independently managed to walk straight past a police cordon without them giving us a second glance.

But our troubles really began on the concourse. Holmes dropped me a wink as we met up again.

"We'll make an actor out of you yet Watson," he said softly. "We're halfway there. Let us stand here for a while and survey the lay of the land for a bit. There may be others in disguise like ourselves, here with the specific purpose of watching for our passing."

He leaned against one of the tall stone pillars while cupping a match to a newly-rolled cigarette. I heard the *pop* an instant before a chip of stone flew less than two inches from Holmes' head, cutting a bloody gouge across his cheek. There was a second *pop* and I felt something *tug* at my sleeve. I had come under fire often enough in my military career to recognize that we were in a dashed sticky situation.

"It seems someone is intent on flushing us out Watson," Holmes said. "Come, it is time we took our leave again."

And without another word he headed off at a weaving run through the crowd. Of course such a thing was always going to attract attention, and the policemen in the entranceway quickly took note. Another *pop* sent a chip of stone flying near my feet, and that was enough to get me moving. I followed Holmes through the crowd.

Another shot *pinged* off the platform at Holmes' feet

and I suddenly realized that we were not heading *away* from the source of the shots, but directly towards it. I looked upwards. A dark figure stood on the high walkway that led to the adjoining platforms, a rifle aimed directly at me, too much in shadow for me to make out his features. I ducked and weaved instinctively and when I looked up again it was to see the figure move further into the shadows until he was completely lost from view.

"Damn," Holmes muttered loudly. "Lost him."

Almost immediately several police whistles echoed around the station and a group of officers headed towards us. They were also blocking any chance of us leaving via the entrance.

"This way Watson," Holmes said, and leapt down onto the tracks. I followed, just yards in front of a train pulling in to the station. Seconds later we were heading at pace along the side of the rails, the full length of the goods train now blocking us off from any pursuit as we left the passenger platform behind.

Holmes led me quickly across the tracks and out of the station to the north. I expected him to double back but instead we headed directly into the dark mouth of one of the tunnels that peppered the area. We moved deep into the shadows and Holmes motioned me to quiet.

Framed by the semi-circle of the tunnel entrance the lights of the station seemed very bright at first until my eyes adjusted. I don't know how long we stood there, but it was more than long enough for me to catch my breath and for my heart rate to slow to a more normal level. There were distant shouts and whistles as the police searched for us in vain. No one approached within a hundred yards of our position.

«««—»»»

SHERLOCK HOLMES: REVENANT

We waited for an hour before slipping quietly out of the tunnel then off the tracks and into the streets to the north of the station. Once at a safe distance we stopped, mainly to allow me to rest my aching leg and share a cigarette with Holmes in the shadow of a tall wall well away from any streetlights.

"We are free, for now," Holmes said, but in truth I felt anything but. I would hax`ve given almost anything at that low point of the night to be back in the comfort of Baker Street, sitting at the fireside with my pipe and a large measure of Scotch. Given our current circumstances I surmised that such relaxation might be rather a long way in my future.

Holmes only allowed us that brief rest stop before setting off again into the night.

Our escape from London proved remarkably simple after the near escape at King's Cross, involving as it did a long walk out towards Barnet before dawn then out into the open country beyond as the sun rose. In all that part of the journey we scarcely passed a soul, and those that we did paid us little heed.

By the end of that first long day a series of lifts from farm carts had taken us north of Watford and we finally took accommodation in a small but busy inn several hours after nightfall. Not a single person in the bar gave us a second glance, although I did take quite a turn on seeing our likeness on the front page of every newspaper. "Wanted for murder," was not something I ever thought to see associated with my name; or with Holmes' for that matter.

I mentioned the fact to Holmes when we were out of range of any possible eavesdroppers.

"Yes, I'm afraid we took the bait all too readily," Holmes said. We were sitting in a quiet corner of the bar, supping on some surprisingly pleasant ale, and I was proving to myself that my cigarette rolling skills had not deserted me even after many years of being out of practice. This was the first Holmes had spoken of the events of the night before since we left Kings Cross and I was eager to hear his thinking on the matter now that he had taken some time mulling it over.

"You are certain it was a deliberate trap?" I asked.

"Oh, most certain," Holmes said, keeping his voice low and even, although I knew of old that the fire in his eyes showed just how angry he had been made. "They played to my curiosity and, I'm afraid, my vanity; knowing exactly what would draw me in. And the fact that there was a gunman waiting, just for us, at King's Cross station tells me that whoever they are, they are highly organized – maybe even enough to have people watching at all the stations out of town last night."

"And do you have any thoughts yet on who *they* might be?"

He was so quiet at that I did not think he would answer, but when he did I realized he had indeed given it thought.

"I do not yet know the who, why or how of it Watson," he said. "But we are up against the highest of intellects; an adversary of particular skill and cunning. I know whom I *might* suspect, were he not already dead. But such questions are futile without more facts on which to base our suppositions. As I have said, the answers lie in Scotland; once there we shall see what we shall see."

He refused to be drawn after that, but I knew that his keen mind was always at work during our long journey north in the days following.

The inn proved to be our last chance of relaxation for some time. We had a hard toil through the Midlands, with few chances of help on the way and long days spent trudging along muddy paths in drizzle and fog. I was thoroughly miserable long before we reached Birmingham.

Our fortunes took a turn for the better thereafter when we made passage on an empty coal barge returning along the canal to Manchester. Although the weather did not improve much, my mood certainly did. We were travelling in the right direction, by a path unwatched by the law, and we were able to partially relax while doing so. My only real problem was maintaining the fiction that I was an itinerant worker and I received some strange looks from the barge owner during the journey, although he said nothing to either myself or Holmes, being happy to take the money Holmes had offered for our freight.

There was only one other matter of note before our investigations in Scotland began, and it happened in Crewe. By then Holmes had decided that we were sufficiently far north that we could risk taking a train the rest of the way. He stayed in the crowd on the northbound platform while I went to get tickets for the Glasgow train. And it was there, while standing in the queue, that I felt someone try to pick my pocket. Or so I thought. But when I put my hand down I felt a single piece of paper there.

"Meet me here," a soft Scots voice said. "I know who has done this to you."

I turned towards the voice, already too late, and caught a glimpse of a small figure part running, part limping away. When I went after him I lost him in the station forecourt and could not risk drawing attention to myself by giving chase at speed or by calling out. I went back to the ticket queue, keeping a close eye for anyone that might have noticed the encounter or might be watching me too closely. No one seemed to be interested. There was a policeman sitting on one of the benches by the door but he was obviously off duty, smoking a pipe and lost in a newspaper. I was able to buy our tickets north with no further ado.

On returning to the platform I showed Holmes the page that had been so deftly placed in my pocket. It was another sheet that looked to have been roughly torn from the same book as the one I had received back in Baker Street.

CALX was the heading. An illuminated drawing showed a young man, bound to a burning wheel by hands and feet in a figure X. He was smiling. Holmes studied it for some time before talking. He rubbed the paper between his fingers as he had done with the previous page.

"It certainly *feels* like it has come from the same source," he said. "And it provides us with more alchemical clues. *Calx* is Latin for Lime. In this case, it is a metaphor for *calcination*, or the process of purifying by heating. If you burn a body hot enough, it goes black, then, if you burn it even hotter, the ash turns white. Similarly, if you heat limestone, you'll produce a white powder that the Romans called *Calx Vita* or quicklime. This was considered a magical material, for, if you poured water on it, it gave out heat. Effectively, giving warmth back to the giver."

"And now I'm afraid I am lost again," I said.

"This one is relatively simple," Holmes replied. "Look at the picture. Fire purifies. It is also a code that says, in effect, make quicklime. It will give heat back to the giver. And, beyond that, it symbolizes the fact that the adept must purify his soul before continuing."

He tapped at the picture.

"It is from Greek mythology. *Ixion* was punished by Zeus. He tried to seduce *Hera*, and for his presumption was bound to a perpetual wheel of fire. But Ixion had seen the face of the Goddess, and although in eternal pain, was also eternally happy. Everything can be seen from two angles. Everything has at least two meanings."

I told Holmes what the vagrant had said, about knowing who our adversary might be, and Holmes smiled.

"And I believe I know where to go to find him," he said, but he took some almost childlike delight in refusing to let me in on his latest secret. "You know me, Watson. I must confirm to my own satisfaction that I am right before I share the information."

Our train arrived shortly afterwards and Holmes went quiet. I thought discussion on the matter was finished for the moment, but once we had a carriage to ourselves he continued.

"What we must ascertain is what part these *gifts* you have received play in this matter. I am of the opinion that they are clues, meant to lead us onwards. But are they part of the solution... or part of the problem? That is the question that vexes me now."

This time he did fall quiet and I smoked in silence for the remainder of the journey.

Chapter Two

Holmes had already intimated that Glasgow was not to be our final destination, but he did not allow me into his confidence until some time after we disembarked at Central Station. Firstly though we had to endure a walk past a small army of police officers, all intent on studying every disembarking passenger.

"It seems we are expected," Holmes whispered as we approached the ticket barrier. "Keep quiet, follow my lead, and be prepared to run if the need arises. There may be another *sniper* trying to flush us out."

I cursed him inwardly for reminding me of the fact, for all his warning achieved was to make me nervous, and I was sure that was going to be obvious to any of the police officers should they decided to take a closer look at us.

The station itself was a noisy confusion of engine noise, smoke and excited passengers but suddenly Holmes' strident voice carried above them all. It was also the most convincing Scots accent I had heard since my time on the line in Afghanistan with Corporal Black from Maryhill.

"So I said to her, 'Get away wi' ye woman and stop talking such tripe,' but ye ken wit women are like? She only went and skelped me ower the heid wi' a pan. I was fair affronted so I was and…"

Much to my amazement he kept on in that vein for several minutes as we reached the head of the queue and handed over our tickets. We walked through the crowded concourse and out into Union Street. No one stopped us, no one shot at us and there were no police whistles in our wake.

Holmes was obviously well pleased with this latest ruse.

"I say old man," I whispered. "Wasn't that a bit of a risk."

He laughed, and half-dragged me across the busy thoroughfare and down a tall shaded alley I would not have entered of my own free will.

"The bigger risk would have been to stay quiet. People see and hear what they expect to see and hear, and in a city like this, they expect the locals to talk, and loudly at that."

He herded me to a tall wooden door. It was only when he pushed it open that I heard the sound of laughter and smelled the smoke and ale. A sign I hadn't previously noticed above the doorway told me what I had come to guess; we were about to enter a public bar, *The Horseshoe*. Holmes had a quick look round to make sure no one was paying any heed to us and ushered me inside.

It turned out to be a large open barn of a place with much mahogany and some particularly fine large painted mirrors. It was also rather busy, but none of the clientele paid us much attention, intent as they were on their own drinking. Holmes walked up to the bar and, still in character, ordered 'two pints of eighty shilling and two pies.' He leaned over and whispered something to the barman. Several white five-pound notes passed from Holmes across the bar and were so quickly taken out of his hand and spirited away in the barman's pocket that I believe I was the only person in the whole place to notice. We were quickly motioned through to a room at the rear of the building that contained little more than two armchairs, a small table and a fireplace. The barman winked at Holmes.

"I'll see to it that you're not disturbed sirs," he said and left us alone.

Holmes immediately relaxed.

"We're clear Watson, for now at least. George will keep any prying eyes away, and we are safer in here than just about any other place in the country."

"Holmes, you never cease to astonish me. You mean you are known, here in this bar?"

Holmes smiled.

"I have had several cases to solve for the industrialists in this fine city, before your time as my *chronicler* of course, but this old place never changes much. And I have found over the years that this particular spot is an excellent central base of operations."

"But it is a public bar," I replied.

"Where better to hear from the public?" Holmes said laughing. "I also have arrangements with several other bar owners across the country. My web of information gathering has numerous strands, and this bar is at one of the junctions. Besides, George knows more than anyone about the doings of the criminal fraternity in this area, having been a pawnbroker of some ill repute before seeing the light and turning his hand to innkeeping."

He took off his overcoat, dropped into one of the chairs and immediately looked as relaxed as if he was back Baker Street. I sat down opposite him and rolled a cigarette for each of us. Minutes later the barman, George I presumed, brought a tray through with the beers and two piping-hot pies. The man left, dropping me another wink as he departed. "I'll be back with some more beer after I've seen to your errands sir," he said to

43

Holmes, and Holmes acknowledged him with a wave.

The pies, although they looked suspiciously gray inside, proved to be delicious and peppery although the meat was unidentifiable, possibly mutton although I could not be sure. Much to my embarrassment I managed to dribble a stream of hot grease down the sleeve of my jacket, which got another laugh from Holmes as I made an unsightly smear while trying to remove it.

"A touch of verisimilitude I had not thought of Watson. I may try it myself."

After eating Holmes took to the ale with relish. To my palate it seemed somewhat heavy on malt and syrup and had too little hop compared to the Fullers' I was used to back in town, but after a while I grew accustomed to the taste and to my surprise polished it off quite rapidly.

"We shall make a Scotsman of you yet Watson," Holmes said and, as if the beer had suddenly loosened his tongue, proceeded to run through his thoughts on the case so far.

"I have been thinking," he said. "And our recent close call at the ticket barrier has firmed up my thoughts. *'People see and hear what they expect to see and hear.'* And therein lies the crux of the matter. Our adversary relied on that fact when he set his trap for me."

He took a proffered cigarette, lit it with a taper from the fireside and sucked on it contentedly before continuing.

"He knew of course that I would be making a close study of everything that happened to the stricken Lords... indeed he counted on it. I draw your attention to the mouth movements in particular. That was a work of some genius."

My confusion must have shown, and Holmes smiled.

"I did not think you had noticed, Watson. According to Mycroft, all of the stricken Lords have been mouthing the same thing... a Latin phrase. *Ab ovo usque ad mala*."

"From eggs to apples. From Horace?"

"Yes, the *Satire*. But it also has been used in several alchemical texts, for the egg is commonly used to symbolize the *macrocosm*, but it also used to denote the beginning of all things, whereas apples represent forbidden knowledge, as in *The Apples of the Hesperides*. But even that is not the most relevant usage in this case. It seems we have a trickster at work against us Watson, for there is yet another place where those same words turn up – in the family motto of the common descendant of the six lords, Angus Seton, Laird of Comrie. I made the connection – I saw what I wanted to see – and thus we were drawn into the trap."

George returned at that moment with two more of the strong beers. I started my second more cautiously, aware that a certain tiredness was setting in to my bones. Starting to relax was potentially dangerous in our current situation, but Holmes seemed to have become settled, at least for now, so I allow myself some laxity and sat back in the chair with a fresh smoke.

"But Holmes," I said. "If it *was* a trap, then surely our opponent will have guessed that we will be searching for an answer here in Scotland?"

Holmes nodded.

"In fact, I am counting on it. Our only hope of clearing our names is to force a confrontation. Even before that, I want to ensure that we are the ones setting any traps from here on. But that is for tomorrow. Tonight, we shall rest up here and let George's contacts do some legwork for us."

What with the ale and the seeping tiredness I was

almost asleep when George returned about an hour later.

"You were right Mister Holmes," he said. "I have an address for you. It is an old Medieval Keep up a farm track in Limehouse."

"This Limehouse... it is where I thought it would be?"

George laughed.

"There's not much gets past you sir. Yes... it is a small hamlet just to the east of Comrie."

Once George left I asked Holmes what the significance of the last conversation had been, but he was again lost in thought and I knew better than to interrupt. George also came back soon afterwards with another two beers but I left mine alone; I had further questions before I could allow myself to sleep. But Holmes would say no more, merely referred me back to the latest piece of paper; the one that had been slipped into my pocket in Crewe.

"Lime-house Watson... I told you it was a clue."

I took out the page and studied the image of the crucified youth, smiling as he burned, but for the life of me I could not see how it applied in any shape or form to our current situation. And at that the tiredness finally took me. I fell into a most welcome slumber.

«««—»»»

I woke some time later, with a stiff back and a sour taste in my mouth of stale tobacco and beer. That was quickly overcome by the smell of freshly buttered toast and tea. George looked almost embarrassed as he put a tray down on the small table. It had been the slight noise he had made on entering that had woken me. Thin sunlight came in through thick dusty curtains – I had slept all night in the chair. Indeed Holmes had not yet wakened, being still asleep on the opposite side of the now-cold fireplace.

"The missus made me get out the best china," George said. "So for God's sake don't break it or I'll be in the doghouse for months."

The *china* was indeed made of particularly fine porcelain but I scarce noticed; I realized I was hungry enough to eat almost anything and I took to the toast with gusto. Holmes woke, stretched and reached for the tobacco pouch on the arm of the chair by his right hand.

"Toast Holmes?"

He shook his head. "Not this morning. We have some travelling to do and I fear my constitution will not permit food yet."

"We are travelling?" I asked between more mouthfuls of toast.

He nodded, and looked up at the barman. "That is, if everything is arranged?"

George nodded back.

"I have a carriage that will take you most of the way – up to Aberfoyle then along the side of the lochs. It is not a short trip, and will take all day, but once out of the city there will be little chance of anyone taking notice of you. Just stay hidden in the carriage for the first hour or so and everything will be smooth as silk."

"In that case," Holmes said, removing his rather threadbare waistcoat. "I believe the time for disguise is over. I trust you managed to secure us a change of clothing?"

This was said to the barman. The man tapped his nose and winked. "Some very nice stuff indeed Mr. Holmes if I say so myself. Just don't ask me which gentleman will be looking for his *troosers* this morning." He laughed loudly. It looked like something he did a lot and I couldn't help raising a smile of my own in reply.

"Dashed good of you sir," I said. "But if I can bother you for one more thing? I need a wash and a shave before I'll be fit to share an enclosed space with anyone."

He showed us to a small washroom at the rear.

As I joined Holmes in starting to wash away the make-up and accumulated grime – which was a dashed difficult job in itself – I asked him if he was certain of this course of action.

He smiled thinly.

"Your limping friend found us in Crewe despite all our attempts at evasion," he said. "And we were spotted easily enough at King's Cross. I don't know about you Watson, but I would rather walk in the light than slink in the darkness. Besides, I am tired of running. It is time we wrested the initiative back in our favor."

I will admit that divesting myself of the guise I had worn these past days did indeed feel liberating, and once washed, shaved and dressed I realized that I felt less like a criminal and more like my old self. The clothes *provided* by the barman certainly helped, being a particularly fine tweed three-piece suit that felt as if it had hardly been worn. Holmes was similarly well dressed, having been given a dark serge suit and matching cape. By the time Holmes handed me a loaded service revolver I was more than ready to make a start on our rehabilitation.

George had a carriage brought right up against the back entrance of the bar and Holmes and I were able to climb aboard without being seen. We were still travelling light, with only our trusty Gladstone bag as company, but once again George proved himself to be a more than gracious host. There was a picnic hamper on the floor of the carriage that on inspection contained several bottles of ale and enough cold pies, bread and cheese to keep us from starving for the day to come.

We did as George had suggested and kept our heads down for more than an hour into the journey, contenting ourselves to smoking in quiet contemplation. My tobacco consumption over recent days was rather higher than I was accustomed to and as a medical man I knew I should be curtailing my use. But I must say I was rather enjoying the old familiarity of rolling my own cigarettes, and was taking some pride in the quality of the final products. Holmes however was lost in one of his reveries and as ever I had no idea what might be occupying his mind. I also knew better than to ask.

After a while Holmes had obviously had enough *confinement* and drew open the curtain from across the door, allowing us access to the view. It was immediately clear that we were already outside the city, being taken through some well-manicured farmland interspersed with the scars of recent mining activity. I leaned out of the window.

"Driver? Could you tell us where we are?"

He didn't even turn round to acknowledge my question. I thought better of asking again, guessing that anyone hired by George would be used to keeping their mouth shut and their mind free of any thoughts as to why they were taking this particular journey. I contented myself with enjoying the view while nibbling on a thick sandwich of bread and cheese.

Holmes chose that moment to enlighten me further as to our destination.

"You asked me why we are headed for Comrie," he started. "The answer lies, as I have already stated, with the common ancestor of the stricken Lords, a certain Angus Seton as I believe I have already said. The old Keep for which we are headed has been the family seat for more than four hundred years, and continues to be so. If there is an answer to be found, I believe it will be there, for the family has a history that points to a study, if not an obsession, with the practice of alchemy."

That gave me a start, but in reality it should not have, for everything we had learned so far had indeed pointed at an *esoteric* background to the case.

Holmes was still talking.

"The Seton family, as far as I could trace, dates itself as far back as the Norman barons of the twelfth century, and seem to have started to rise in favor as trusted servants to minor scions of Scottish royalty around that time. It is also told, although it is probably apocryphal, that the alchemical obsession began early, as a result of an encounter with an Arabian practitioner during the Third Crusade. What is beyond dispute is that the Seton family have been responsible for many of what are now regarded as definitive texts in the Great Quest."

"I will admit," I said. "It is not a matter that I have given much consideration."

Holmes smiled again.

"Yes, and yet no, Watson. For any study of basic chemistry you have undertaken in the course of your medical education was, as you well know, founded in alchemical practices in its earliest history. Robert Boyle himself was known to be a dabbler in the Quest, as was Isaac Newton."

I did indeed know of the history, but as yet I could not see its application to our current predicament, and I told Holmes so in no uncertain terms.

"That is exactly the reason why we are here Watson. Now I suggest you try to get some rest. I fear we have a night of burglary and adventure ahead of us."

And that was that for a number of hours. The carriage stopped at an old stone coach house at what I took to be the driver and the horses' lunchtime. Holmes and I decided discretion was the better part of valor and stayed hidden. We were however well enough served for our own repast, having a bottle of ale and plenty to eat in the provided hamper. We finished off all of the food that George had provided and I was feeling quite heartened as we started off again, having almost forgotten that we were fugitives from justice.

The remainder of the journey only served to further remove me from our predicament as we traveled through some marvelous highland scenery of forest, high hills and tranquil lochs, barely seeing another living soul in the course of a full afternoon. Holmes remained lost in introspection, our only conversation coming from the occasional request for me to roll him a new cigarette.

Dusk was starting to fall when the carriage came to a halt.

"Limehouse, gentlemen." Those were the only words I had heard from the man all day and as we disembarked he added more, almost as terse. "Shall I wait?"

Holmes sent him away.

"We shall make our own way from here, but thank you," he said. "And thank George for all his help."

The driver nodded and without another word left, leaving Holmes and I standing in a quiet country lane at a junction with a long narrow driveway that seemed to lead up into the low hills beyond. Holmes lifted the Gladstone bag and immediately made for the driveway.

"I promised you some burglary Watson. It seems the time is upon us. Tonight we shall start the process of regaining our good name."

<<<<—>>>>

Reaching the Keep proved to be a rather strenuous

climb of some fifteen minutes, by the end of which I was wishing we had not dismissed the carriage quite so readily. It was also becoming dark and without the benefit of any street lighting I found it difficult to make out the path ahead.

Holmes seemed unperturbed.

"A fine night for our nefarious purposes," he said, and strode on. It was only a minute or so after that we reached the Keep. It seemed to loom up out of nowhere in the gathering gloom so that we were most suddenly confronted with a high stone edifice. It looked to be little more than a tall box, foursquare and solid with only two smallish windows on the side we faced. Walking round to our right brought us in front of a very imposing oak door some eight feet high and firmly locked when I tried it.

"We're not getting in there without an axe," I whispered. "And even then it would take a month of Sundays."

Holmes didn't reply. His attention was already on a small window to the side of the door. He lit a succession of matches while examining the lock and I had to look away from each bright flare to avoid blinding myself. When I looked back after the last match-strike Holmes already had the window open and was clambering inside. When I tried to follow him I found that my frame was too large to squeeze through the narrow gap. I could not see Holmes in the darkness beyond, but I heard him laugh quietly.

"I must have a word with Mrs. Hudson about the size of your breakfasts," he said. "Wait there. I will open the door."

The heavy oak door swung open seconds later. There was an accompanying creak so loud that it disturbed a pair of crows out of the trees, sending them cawing overhead.

"Don't worry about noise old man. It seems we have the run of the place," Holmes said, not bothering to whisper. "The whole Keep is dark and quiet. Cold too - I doubt there has been anyone here in weeks."

He showed me into what felt like a tall hallway judging by the hollow echoes all around us although it was hard to tell exactly, so complete was the darkness. Holmes soon rectified that by finding a tall candle that he took down from a wall sconce. He lit it from a match, and used the light to find several others like it which were ranked at regular intervals along the walls. I saw the light reflecting in the windows at the far end of the hall, and realized that it would be able to be seen from the outside.

"I say Holmes, do you think that is wise? Someone might take note."

"Given our location, I think that unlikely," Holmes said. "Besides, it is a necessary risk if we are to be successful in our efforts. Come, let us see if there is anything here to help us."

I followed him as we made a round of the ground floor of the Keep. As Holmes had already guessed, it was apparent that the place had not been inhabited for some time. Fine dust lay everywhere, spiders had made webbing in most of the corners, and scurrying noises in the dark told of rodents, whether rats or mice I was unable to determine.

The only sign of any human activity at all was in a small library. Holmes lit a pair of oil lamps he found on a console table to show a very well appointed little room. I would have been more than happy to spend my evenings in such a place, with its aged oak paneling, tall bookshelves and wide stone fireplace. Papers lay strewn across a fine mahogany desk, and these became the focus of Holmes' investigation. I perused the volumes on the shelves but their titles were unknown to me. There was obviously an esoteric bent to the content; *The Mysteries of the Wurm, The Twelve Concordances of the Red Serpent* and further titles in Latin, Greek and German that seemed to allude to an alchemical origin. I was about to remark on the fact when I heard Holmes gasp.

I turned to see him have to grasp the edge of the desk to keep from falling. His face was ashen and his eyelids fluttered as if a faint was coming on. I moved over quickly and lent him my shoulder to steady him. When he spoke it was in a whisper.

"Thank you Watson," he said. He waved a sheaf of papers at me. "It was these letters that did it. I fear this matter is more complex than I originally thought. I have been given somewhat of a shock."

"I can see that old man," I said. "Stay here. I'll see if there's any Scotch lying around."

A voice I recognized came from the library doorway.

"I'm afraid your drinking days are over Doctor."

Inspector Lestrade stood in the doorway, with two bulky officers that I did not recognize behind him.

"It seems we will be adding breaking and entering to your charge list," the Inspector said. "Lord Crawford said that this is where we would find you. Your little plot has been foiled, Holmes."

Holmes laughed. He still looked as white as a sheet, but Lestrade's appearance seemed to have taken his mind off whatever had troubled him – for the moment at least.

"And which plot would that be Lestrade?" Holmes said. "Surely you know me better than that? Crawford is the man you need to look at here, not Watson and myself."

Lestrade looked tired and irritable, and was obviously in no mood for any games. It was almost possible to feel some sympathy for the man.

"All I know is that a Lord of the Realm says you threw another Lord of the Realm out of a window in the Houses of Parliament. I cannot find anyone who saw another person in the dead Lord's room, there is no suicide note, and you ran from the scene; both of you. Now come quietly gentlemen. You'll get a fair trial; you know that I am a man of my word on that score. But that is all I can offer you."

Holmes casually shoved the sheaf of letters he held into an inside pocket as if it was the most natural thing in the world and stood straight. I could see the tension rise in him; he was readying himself for action. My hand found the butt of the service revolver in my pocket, but I already knew that I would not be leveling it at the policemen – that would be the step too far. If it came to having to fight with Lestrade in order to escape I decided I would throw myself on the mercy of the law.

"Ask yourself Lestrade," Holmes said. "How did Crawford know to find us here? I myself did not know this would be our destination until early this morning. For you to get here as quickly as you have means that Crawford knew we were coming a long time before we knew it ourselves. How do you think he managed that?"

Lestrade sighed.

"Don't tax me Mr. Holmes. I'm a long way from home and I'm tired. My job is to take you in for questioning. I'll leave it to the legal chaps to sort out the niceties. Now are you coming quietly or not?"

"Not," a Scottish voice said from the hallway beyond. The two officers behind Lestrade shuffled past him into the library, raising their hands above their head. We saw why seconds later when a small man dressed in rags walked into the room; my *friend* from Baker Street and Crewe Railway Station. He carried the largest shotgun I have ever seen – from my close range it looked more like a small cannon. He motioned with it, pointing Lestrade over towards where the two other officers now stood at the fireplace.

"Now Inspector," the man said. "Unless you have a warrant from a Scottish court, I believe it is *you* who are trespassing here. I am probably within my rights as the *Laird* to shoot you first and answer questions later, but I am feeling generous tonight. I believe I will detain you until the law can be brought up here."

"We *are* the law," Lestrade said, and made to move forward. Seton stopped him by pointing the shotgun straight at his chest.

"Doctor Watson," the newcomer said turning to me. "You will find some lengths of rope in the cupboard under the stairs in the hall. Could you fetch them please?"

Holmes laughed.

"It seems my *wee plot* isn't quite ready to roll over and die just yet," he said to Lestrade. "When you have got the time, I suggest you look into a shooting in King's Cross Station on the night of the supposed *murder*. And ask yourself Lestrade, who do we both know that employed a high velocity air gun? If you find the gunman from that scene, I would suggest you will be closer to the actual culprit."

I left them to it.

"You are just making things worse for yourself," Lestrade said. "Any sympathy I might have had for your predicament is rapidly fading. I don't take too kindly to being held at gunpoint."

Seton laughed.

"Maybe you should have thought of that before

entering a Scotsman's house without a warrant."

I heard all of this from the hallway before moving to the under-stairs cupboard where I did indeed find several lengths of stout rope among sundry country items including a particularly fine pair of salmon rods and another shotgun. I considered, only for a second, taking that weapon, but there were already too many guns in there, and if I hadn't been prepared to use a pistol I certainly was not about to menace Lestrade with a *cannon*.

When I returned to the library the Scotsman motioned with the gun again towards the trio of policemen.

"Tie them up please Doctor. Nothing too fancy; just enough to give us time to make our escape."

I did as I was bid, although with some trepidation.

"Don't do it," Lestrade said.

"Sorry about this Inspector," I said. "But as Holmes has explained, we are innocent of the charges against us. We just need a chance to prove it."

"You are not doing yourself any favors here Doctor," Lestrade replied as I bound his hands. "We only have you as an accessory at the moment, but aiding and abetting means you are definitely throwing your career away here."

"I'll take my chances with Holmes," I said.

Lestrade was red in the face with anger. He strained at his bonds, but I had tied him quite securely.

"Just make sure he doesn't throw *you* out of a window Doctor. You know how he is when he gets in a mood."

Holmes laughed bitterly.

"I will remind you of that when I present you with the truth of the matter," he said. "But for now, it is we who have the upper hand. I will see you again soon enough Lestrade, and next time it is I who will have the answers, and you who shall have to provide an apology."

I finished tying up the other policemen's hands, then I bound all three together by looping the longest stretch of rope in four tight rings around them. Lestrade continued to struggle.

"I'll have you locked up on bread and water for the rest of your life for this Watson," he said. "You have my promise on that."

The look in his eye convinced me he was telling the truth, but Holmes and I were too far in now for me to back down. Our only hope seemed to lie with the small Scotsman.

Once satisfied the bonds would hold Seton finally put down the weapon.

"Thank you Doctor, it's a heavy beast to have to lug around. I had best leave it here, for we have a bit of travelling ahead of us. Are you ready for a run on the hills?"

Without further explanation he left the room, obviously expecting us to follow. Holmes didn't hesitate. He picked up the Gladstone bag and handed it to me.

"Come Watson. There are answers waiting for us."

The three of us ran out into the night.

«««—»»»

We did not go far. Having heard the Scotsman's words inside I was fully expecting to have to lug the Gladstone bag over hill and moor with Lestrade and his men in pursuit at our heels. Instead he led us quickly round to the rear of the Keep. There was just enough light from the windows to show us a set of steps leading down into the ground.

"A wee present from my ancestors," the Scotsman whispered. "They too liked to hide things from the authorities."

As he turned away I heard him start to mutter to himself, and I remembered our first encounter. The cadence seemed exactly the same, and this time I could make out the words; a form of Gaelic if I wasn't mistaken, the meaning of which entirely eluded me.

We went deep into the ground to what at first looked to be no more than a chamber for grain storage. He led us, almost blind in the dark, to the rear and slid a panel aside. He lit an oil lamp, the light almost blinding until our eyes adjusted and we saw more steps going down beyond. Sliding the panel shut he then led us further into the depths, into what proved to be a warren of tunnels. As we passed entrances I saw barrels of ale and wine, and boxes, obviously imported from the Orient, that looked never to have been opened.

Before I had time for further investigation the passageway opened into a wider chamber. The air felt fresher here and there was the slightest of breezes. The strangest thing of all however was the diagram that had been painted on the floor. A five-pointed star sat inside three concentric circles. Around the outermost ring ran a series of what looked to my untrained eye to be Arabic hieroglyphs, and along the inner track was painted an inscription in Gaelic. As the Scotsman started to mutter again I realized that he was muttering the words that were written on the floor.

"*Ri linn dioladh na beatha, Ri linn bruchdadh na falluis, Ri linn iobar na creadha, Ri linn dortadh na fala.*"

The Scotsman saw me looking and stopped.

"It may seem like a lot of *hocus-pocus* to you Doctor but I assure you it is necessary for my protection," he said. "I will explain soon enough."

Two rough high-backed benches sat either side of the fireplace and the Scotsman bade us sit as he first lit and stoked a fire, then left us as he went to search for something in a side chamber. I realized that Holmes had not spoken since we left the Keep above. He no longer looked like he might faint, but his face was still pale and his brow was etched with what might have been concentration had it not looked so much like worry.

"Are you quite well old chap?" I asked.

"Nothing a smoke will not cure Watson," he said, and managed a weak smile. I did not get a chance to question him further, for our host returned at that moment carrying a whisky bottle and three glasses. He had also had a change of clothes and a wash that quite transformed him. The rags had gone to be replaced by a fine tweed suit, and a pair of clean shoes covered his feet. The mere act of having combed his unruly mop of red hair and tying it back with a bow meant that we could see his face clearly for the first time. He had the brightest blue eyes I have seen, a wide smile and his teeth were straight and white. He acknowledged my obvious consternation with a grin.

"Well met again Doctor. I am right sorry for the subterfuge, and I assure you it was necessary. When we met before you were not the only one in disguise. But if I am to tell my story then we'll need a dram or two, for it might take a wee while."

So it was Holmes and I sat there deep under a Scottish Keep, sipping whisky, smoking my hastily rolled cigarettes and listening to the most outlandish tale that had ever reached our ears.

«««—»»»

"First things first," he began. "We have not yet been formally introduced."

He took a cigarette from me when I proffered and he

used a long taper lit from the fire to get it going, puffing smoke contentedly before continuing.

"My name is Angus Seton and I am what you might call the master of this fine place. As you are aware by now, my family is regarded as experts in some esoteric fields of research and have been involved in the study of occult practices for many centuries. My own story in so far as it concerns your predicament starts seven years ago, and involves the search for one strand of that knowledge."

He took a long sip from the whisky, which I must admit was remarkable stuff, being peaty, fiery and smooth all at once, and giving one a warm internal glow that lasted long after the liquor had passed the lips. I had to watch what I was doing as it would have been all too easy to take a dive into that particular bottle.

"I received a letter that summer," Seton continued. "It came from Durham, from the University, and showed a great deal of knowledge and erudition. The initial inquiry was regarding the Philosopher's Stone but the writer, over the course of several dozen letters, ranged widely over a variety of topics. It became apparent that he not only knew my family history, but also that he was particularly interested in the areas of research that related to the transmigration of souls.

"Now I myself have always been a practical man, believing that the final goal of the research in the Seton family history was mainly a matter purely of chemistry; that longevity was a goal that could be achieved with the right combination of chemical compounds and experimentation. But the letter writer proposed a more *spiritual* path, one where immortality of the body could be fused with an illuminated mind to produce what he called *the perfect man.* I disagreed with him of course, but his letters were so informed, so erudite, that I could

SHERLOCK HOLMES: REVENANT

not help but be impressed.

"We went backwards and forwards, corresponding for several years. He was obviously proceeding apace with his own experimentation, and I sensed a growing excitement in his writings; he believed he was close to achieving his goal.

"Then, in the spring of ninety-one, the letters suddenly stopped."

Holmes twitched at that, as if he had been given a fresh shock, but when I looked his way he dismissed me with a wave of the hand, and indicated to Seton that he should continue. The Scotsman took the break in his tale as a chance to refill our glasses, and I for one was not about to turn down more of that fine liquor. I sipped at it, savoring the heat that in some ways was even more comforting than that being given out from the fire. Sitting here in the Highlands on such a night one could well see how the *uisque* came to become so much a part of the local's life. I pulled myself out of the momentary reverie; our host had started up his tale from where he left off.

"There were no more letters after the spring of ninety-one," Seton continued. "But I was to find he was far from finished with me. And here my tale becomes passing strange and I fear it might seem most unusual, if not completely outlandish, but please bear with me. I promise you it is pertinent to your current predicament.

"I had quite forgotten my correspondence with the gentleman beyond occasionally wondering why the letters had stopped coming. I was soon to wish I could forget him completely.

"It started in the summer of ninety-four. I was sitting in my study going over a passage in *The Concordances* when the first attack came. It manifested itself as little more than a bad headache at first, then as a crushing pressure inside my skull such that I felt my head might implode. All at once I felt a presence, an obviously alien *thing* creeping through my mind, and it was only with the full force of my will that I was able to repel it. And somehow I knew the source of the attack; my correspondent had indeed found a means to migrate his soul. The trouble was, he was trying to migrate his essence into my body – and I was still the resident."

I was finding Seton's tale more and more difficult to follow, possibly a result of the Scotch, but more likely because it had slipped into the area of the esoteric with which I was completely unfamiliar and if truth be told more than a tad skeptical of. I was about to voice my feelings when Holmes put a hand on my shoulder.

"Let us hear him out Watson," he said. "I believe we need to."

Seton nodded. "That you do and I shall get to the point soon enough. But first, let me go back to those early attacks on me in ninety-four. As I have said, by some means unknown to me consciously, I knew that the source of the attack was the letter writer in Durham. I did not at first understand why, but since then I have developed a theory that I shall get to in good time. However my family has not studied arcane maters all these centuries for no return, and I was quickly able to mount a defense using a Gaelic chant from deep antiquity. Using that, and utilizing the power of the pentacle that you have already seen on the floor, I was able to keep the attacks at bay."

I believe I let out a disbelieving *harrumph* at that, but Seton did not seem to take offense. He continued after a long sip of his Scotch.

"Doctor Watson here has already spotted that I am prone to muttering the protection spell at inopportune moments, but I assure you it is most necessary, for the attacks are strong and frequent. Back then at the start they came even faster, but when it became apparent that I was not about to succumb, the man in Durham – which is how I always thought of him for I never learned his name – changed tack. Having failed with me, he took to making attempts on people with the same bloodline... my family.

"My first intimation of this came at a wedding. Young John, a nephew barely twenty-three and full of life, was so happy at his betrothal to a sweet lass from Dunfermline. After the vows we all went to the Church Hall for the dancing. John came over, shook my hand and looked me in the eye. The change came on him fast; his mouth went slack, his eyes went dead and he started to mouth soundless words. Then, mere seconds later, he fell, stone dead in my arms."

Seton paused to wipe away a sudden tear before continuing.

"He was only the first of many. Over that first year I lost ten family members, all male, all cut off in the prime of life. And all the same way according to the reports of those present at the deaths. At the same time the attacks on me continued apace and I was sorely weakened through having to constantly defend myself. I decided that I could not wait for everyone I knew and loved to die around me, so I went looking for the source.

"I traveled to Durham in hope, but it ended in despair, for I had scarcely been there an hour when I discovered that the man I sought was dead – perished in May of ninety-one."

I believed I was starting to see where this was going, and I did not like the thought, not one bit. And as ever, Holmes had been ahead of me for some time. He took the sheaf of letters from his pocket.

"I knew it as soon as I saw your letters," Holmes

said. "I would know that hand anywhere, despite the lack of a signature."

He handed the papers to me. My eye was immediately drawn to the overelaborate letter inscribed at the bottom of the top one.

A single letter.

M... for Moriarty.

Chapter Three

I was so dumbfounded I was unable to speak for several seconds, and Holmes was lost in thought staring into the fire and chewing on a cigarette. Seton filled the empty space.

"Yes Mr. Holmes. As you have surmised it was indeed Professor Moriarty with whom I was in correspondence, although I did not know it myself until my trip to Durham. And I now believe that you can piece most of the rest of the tale together for yourself. Moriarty's body may have perished at those Falls where you so nearly met your doom, but his spirit lives on. It lives on, and it is looking for a body to inhabit permanently. My body to be precise."

I recognized Holmes' expression.

Something does not ring true.

He gave voice to it before I could.

"And Moriarty, having returned from the Great Beyond, has decided to spend his immortality in having some sport with myself and some distant relatives of yours in the House of Lords while waiting for you to stop fighting him? Is that your story?"

Seton did not reply. He and Holmes appraised each other for long seconds, like two old dogs deciding whether a fight was worth the effort. In the end Holmes' iron will won through, and Seton sighed deeply.

"I should have known better than to try to outfox Sherlock Holmes," he said. "But I have not lied to you –

merely been rather economical with the truth. For, you see, I was afraid you might not listen to my tale if I told you Moriarty's real goal."

"Which is?" Holmes asked.

Seton drank almost a full glass of Scotch before replying, and when he did speak it was in the most matter-of-fact manner that made his subsequent statement all the more incredible.

"There is a specific reason why he wants my body in particular. When I said my *family* has been researching in the arcane for many centuries, I was not quite accurate. I really should have said that *I* have been. I was born in the year Fourteen Eighty Three, in Port Seton near Edinburgh, and I know the secret of immortality."

««(—»»

Of course, that kind of thing is a bit of a conversation stopper. Holmes recovered his composure before I did.

"You are right of course; such a statement does raise more questions than answers. But if you ask me to believe that Moriarty's spirit is still *somewhere* in the ether looking for a body, then it is but a small leap of deduction from that to believing the totality of the tale. And I have a feeling that if we are to resolve this matter then we must proceed as if what you say is true, until proven otherwise."

"But alchemy is nothing but gibberish and gobbledygook," I said. "I know, I've tried to read some of the manuscripts, back when I was a student and much more fanciful."

"Gibberish," Seton said, pouring himself yet another whisky. "Even that word has an alchemical history. The word comes from the name of an Eighth Century Islamic alchemist, Jabir ibn Hayyan, the same man who described the making of the stained glass. His name was Latinized as *Geber*. He wrote in a mangled verse that was so convoluted and strange that it coined the word. And since him, alchemists have always hidden their secrets in code."

"You mean all that nonsense about pelicans and pheasants actually means something?"

"Well in most texts, the pelican is shown stabbing its breast with its beak and nourishing its young with its own blood. It symbolizes self-sacrifice and the abandonment of worldly things with no thought of consequence. But the pelican is also the name for a piece of apparatus. Double, and even triple, meanings abound. Even after you had deciphered the code, you would still have to struggle through all the possible symbolic meanings to get to the heart of it and find the truth."

"And you are claiming you did?"

Seton nodded in agreement.

"Although there is no way right now for me to prove it to you beyond reciting history that only someone who has lived it would know. Can you just trust me in this Doctor? For tonight at least?"

I owed him *something* for his whisky. I raised a glass in agreement and he continued.

"As soon as I heard of the maladies afflicting the Lords I knew Moriarty was up to some mischief; but the nature of that plot escapes me even now. I do not believe it was done solely for the purpose of having you put under suspicion."

"Agreed," Holmes said. "Although it must suit his purposes to have me out of London for a while."

Holmes turned to me.

"Well, old friend. It seems we are deep in those murky waters I mentioned a while back. What say you? Shall we return to London and clear our names?"

"Certainly," I replied. "Although I don't know how that can be managed."

"Neither do I," Holmes said and laughed. "But with an immortal at our side how can we fail?"

Seton joined in the laughter. For a while we had quite forgotten our predicament, but we were brought back to earth with a bump when Seton motioned us to be quiet. Somewhere above us we heard shouting, as if coming from a far distance.

"Just keep quiet for a minute or two," Seton said. "It seems the Scotland Yard boys have finally slipped their bonds. But they'll never find us here. They think we're off and running in the hills, mark my words."

The sounds soon faded, leaving us sitting in silence. It seemed that Seton had been right in his assessment of the policemen's actions.

"Now gentlemen," Seton said once we were sure everything would stay quiet. "My cards are on the table. I know that I would like to take the attack to the bugger. How about you? Are you serious about returning to London and bearding the lion in his den?"

"Perfectly serious," Holmes replied. "I am tired of slinking in shadows. I would like to make a triumphant entrance if possible, but with Lord Crawford's testimony hanging over our heads I do not see how it can be done."

Seton smiled.

"That is something I may be able to help with."

«««—»»»

Seton left us for several minutes and returned dragging some heavy manacles and chains behind him.

"This old castle hasn't needed these for many years," he said. "But they may prove useful tonight."

He half-carried, half-dragged the chains over to the

pentacle on the floor.

"I have been experimenting with a means to take the fight to my attacker," Seton said. "But I have been wary about trying it without someone here to help me in case it goes wrong. Tonight is the perfect opportunity, and might be the only chance we get."

He stepped completely into the pentacle and locked himself into the manacles.

"These chains will wrap twice around my body, if you would be so kind Doctor?"

I did as I was bidden, wrapping him in the chains, the weight of which almost buckled his knees. He sat down hard on the floor and nodded.

"Perfect. Even if he gets control of my body he will be unable to do much about it."

"If who gets control?" I asked, but I already knew the answer to that. Seton ignored me and looked towards Holmes.

"You knew the man. Will you be able to keep him talking for a while? If we can distract him, then I may be able to do some good at the other end in London."

Holmes nodded.

"I see. You plan to give him an opening so to speak – allow him into your body while you switch into Lord Crawford? I must admit to being baffled as to the how of this matter, but I shall take your word that it is possible. If it is Moriarty's spirit that turns up, I am sure we shall find plenty to talk about," Holmes said dryly.

Seton laughed. He seemed to do that more than any other man I have ever met, so much so that I had started to wonder if he wasn't actually quite mad.

"I never said it was possible," the Scotsman said. "I only said that I would try. I do not think the idea that I can emulate his trick has crossed Moriarty's mind, but if it has, he might be prepared for it and all that will happen is that I will sit on this cold floor for a while. We shall see what we shall see. Help yourself to my *uisque* gentlemen. This could prove to take a while as we need to wait until he renews his attack."

With that he fell quiet, sitting inside the pentacle with his eyes closed.

"I say Holmes," I whispered. "You are not taking any of this nonsense seriously are you?"

Holmes took so long to reply I thought he might be ignoring the question, and when he did reply it was in deadly earnest.

"I saw much on my travels in the East that has taught me never to underestimate the power inherent in the human will," he said. "And if anyone had the strength of will to pierce the veil of death, then surely Mortiarty is that man? At this point in proceedings, I am keeping an open mind, and I suggest you do the same Watson."

The absurdity of our situation did not escape me. We were somewhere deep under a Scottish Keep, with Lestrade looking for us overhead, watching a man who claimed to be immortal sitting inside a pentagram, wrapped in chains.

"We are rather far from the fireside in Baker Street," I said to myself.

Holmes chuckled.

"But at least we can still have a smoke."

I rolled us a cigarette each and we smoked in silence, all the while having an occasional glance towards the pentagram. Seton had been so quiet I thought he might be asleep but just as I reached the last puff of my cigarette, the Scotsman's body started to twitch violently as if he was having a seizure. I got off the bench, thinking to go to his aid, but Holmes held me back.

"No Watson. I think it has begun. Let me do any talking that is required."

««—»»

Seton started to struggle ever more violently, but the chains held and he was unable to move. His head came up slowly and when he saw Holmes he smiled broadly.

"You have come further than I thought," he said. It was the same clipped English voice I had heard Crawford use back in Parliament, and it was quite a shock to the system to hear it again coming from the Scotsman's mouth. "And I see you have made some preparations in the event of my success."

He rattled the chains theatrically.

"What say you Holmes? Is this not my most creative endeavor thus far?"

Holmes made a long slow play of stubbing out his cigarette in the grate before replying.

"It is certainly a very creative act Mister Seton. You must have spent a long time in Moriarty's company to be able to mimic the voice so accurately. I particularly like the way you have captured the slight Northern accent that the man himself struggled so hard to hide. Leeds if I'm not mistaken?"

The chained figure – I cannot bring myself to call him Moriarty – laughed.

"Come Holmes, that is beneath even you. What would Seton have to gain by such deception? And does Seton know that you had a glass of whisky in one hand and a pipe in the other when you allowed a peer of the realm to leap out of a window? What about you Watson – did I not call you *the faithful dog?* Did you forget that?"

Holmes waved a hand. "Parlor tricks do not impress

me. Moriarty was a man of science. He would not stoop to the pretense of the existence of some kind of afterlife."

The sitting figure laughed again.

"If it is proof you want you only have to take your own life; it is the simplest thing. A touch too much morphine should do it painlessly enough – certainly with less drama than throwing yourself off a waterfall."

He rattled the chains again.

"But come Holmes. Surely you have questions of me? Will you not attempt to uncover my plans? Will there be no dramatic pronouncements of how I will be caught and brought to justice? I think you'll find some difficulty in that area."

"If it is the matter in London of which you speak," Holmes said. "Lestrade is already convinced of our innocence in any wrongdoing. It is a misunderstanding; that is all Mister Seton. If you are seeking to profit from our discomfort I am afraid you will have a long wait."

The man in the pentacle laughed again.

"You mean to keep up this pretense? Very well then, so be it. But remember this night Holmes. There will come a time, and it will be soon, when you may wish you had asked more questions of me."

Holmes raised an eyebrow.

"I have learned all I need to know about you Seton; you are a liar and a charlatan, merely trying to profit from our reduced circumstances."

The sitting man's lips turned up in a snarl.

"Admit it Holmes, this time I have bested you."

It was Holmes' turn to laugh.

"And pray tell me," he said. "Which of us is currently sitting in chains?"

This time the chain rattling was not done for dramatic effect but was a serious attempt to test the strength of the bonds. It did not last long – the iron was old, but it was strong, and it held.

Holmes laughed again.

"Nice try Mister Seton, but I am afraid you have not got the accent quite right. Besides, it has been several years since I killed Moriarty. Why would he return now?"

The sitting figure went still, lifted his head and smiled.

"Why indeed? Now we come to the question you *really* want to ask. But why should I help you with clues? No Holmes, you have much work to do if you are to stop me this time. I have the upper hand, and you are a fugitive from justice. I will be there to watch you hang," the sitting man said, then, as if a switch had been thrown, his head fell forward and the body slumped. This time when I moved to Seton's aid Holmes did not stop me.

Seton's eyes rolled up in their sockets and he fell in a dead faint, his head hitting the stone floor hard. It took me far too long to get him out of the chains and I had a bad moment or two when I thought he might have died on me, but when we got him over to the fire it became apparent he was still breathing. For how much longer that would be the case I was not entirely sure, for his heart was thudding so fast I thought his chest might burst. He breathed in short sharp gasps, and when he sat up suddenly and screamed I dashed near had a seizure myself.

"Whisky," he whispered. As a medical man I should have said no, but I had a feeling that my medical skills were not actually required. I was proved right seconds later when, after a slug of liquor that might have floored a horse, he was breathing regularly and his heartbeat had slowed to a walking pace. It took him several

SHERLOCK HOLMES: REVENANT

minutes after that however before he felt able to talk.

"I will not be doing that again in a hurry," he said. "But even if you did not learn anything at this end, I think you will find it was worthwhile when I tell you my tale." With that he stood, shakily at first, then with more confidence. "But I shall have to make haste, for you need to get out of here. Our opponent now knows where you are and, given his position, will surely use the information sooner rather than later. You must be off, and quickly."

Holmes had said nothing since the man's collapse in the pentacle, and he still did not speak, leaving it to me to voice my concerns.

"I cannot leave you man," I said. "You may look as strong as an ox, but I know just how close to death's door you have just come."

Seton smiled.

"I plan on being around a wee while longer Doctor, you may have no fear on that score. But we must split up, for he may attack at any time, and now that he has had access once, it may be easier for him from now on. I cannot chance giving him your location each time."

Holmes finally spoke.

"I can see the logic in that," he said. "And I sense the urgency. So, quickly Seton, tell me what you have learned."

<<<<—>>>>

"I do believe I was nearly lost completely," Seton said while filling a pipe from a tobacco box on the mantelpiece. "I drifted somewhere in a black infinity that was almost peaceful. Shadows drifted with me and some even tried to speak, but the voices were faint and indistinct, like shouts heard from a distance through a strong wind. The feeling of kinship, of brotherhood with those shadows was almost overpowering."

He paused, and seemed almost wistful before getting back on subject.

"But that part can wait for more a more conducive time, and after I myself have had time to think on the ramifications of what I experienced there. I shall attempt to stick to the important aspects of my experience. I was in that blackness for a *long* time. After what seemed an eternity I opened my eyes to look into a well-appointed office space. I realized that this must be Lord Crawford's office in the Lords, a room that I believe the good Doctor here is familiar with?"

He went on without waiting for a reply.

"I knew that I might not have much time, and indeed as it turns out I only just managed to complete the tasks. But I did accomplish three things, all of which are pertinent. My first step was to write a letter to Inspector Lestrade, saying that I had recanted my previous statement and that Sherlock Holmes did not in fact kill anyone. It was scrawled rather hastily, and it will not get you off completely of course, but it should sow sufficient confusion to buy you some time.

"I sealed the letter and took it out into the corridor where I made sure the young policeman there knew both what its contents were and to whom it should be delivered. His testimony to our conversation should also lead to further confusion."

Seton had finally got his pipe lit to his satisfaction and was puffing away merrily. He showed no signs that he had been near death just minutes before. I still doubted he was immortal, but he did seem to have a truly remarkable constitution.

"I have saved the last pieces of information for last," he continued. "For I am unsure of their import. As I was acutely aware that my time might be short I returned to the Lord's office and started to go through the items on his desk, in the hope that there might be some indication of his plans.

"I found a note from the Home Secretary asking for recommendations on dealing with *'the current Irish situation'*, a large file which contained detailed diagrams and costing for the building of the new Central London underground line, and a railway timetable for the Fenchurch Street to Southend line. Make of that what you will."

"Is there anything else you remember?" Holmes asked.

Seton shook his head.

"I was about to start on the desk drawers when I felt something *tug* at me. The next thing I knew I was back here struggling for breath and in urgent need of *uisque*."

Holmes went quiet again and took on a look that I knew meant a long period of contemplation was looming; one that we scarce had time for. Seton had also spotted Holmes' silence.

"I was serious when I said you must leave... and quickly," Seton reminded us. "I need to stay here, but I will do all I can to help. I may even be able to come to your aid at an opportune moment if the chance arises."

Seton suddenly seemed imbued with a sense of purpose. He led us back up out of the underground tunnels and made us wait in the shadows while he checked that the police were indeed gone. We then made our way quickly back into the small library where we had left Lestrade and the others – there was no sign of them bar some lengths of rope left lying on the floor. The shotgun was still leaning against the wall where Seton had left it earlier.

Seton saw me looking at the weapon.

"Do not even consider taking that with you," he said

with a grin. "You'll do yourself a mischief before you get a hundred yards lugging that beast. Let's get you something more useful shall we?"

Twenty minutes later we were on our way down the dark driveway. I carried the Gladstone bag; heavier now, having gained some food and ale to help us on the journey. Before leaving I tried to persuade Seton to reconsider and join us, but he had already retreated back into a muttering reverie and even as we said goodbye at the door of the Keep he was reciting his litany.

I turned and gave one last wave, but he did not acknowledge it and was soon lost from sight in the gloom.

Chapter Four

Dawn broke to find us walking along a high moorland road somewhere south of Comrie on a path that Holmes informed me would eventually bring us to the outskirts of Dunblane and thence south to Kincardine where we would finally be able to cross the Forth. I was glad to be with someone with knowledge of the geography for, apart from the salmon runs of the Tweed and the Dee, I had little sense of my way around Scotland outside the cities.

Holmes seemed thoughtful but in good spirits, which is more than could be said for myself. I was finding it hard to come to terms with what I had witnessed in the chamber under the Keep, and daylight brought with it a return to some kind of rational thinking on my part. The more the sun rose, the more the events took on a dream like quality and I began to suspect that we had been hoodwinked completely by a master illusionist.

I explained my misgivings to Holmes, expecting the great rationalist himself to agree with me, but to my astonishment he held to a completely opposite viewpoint.

"No Watson," he said. "I have no doubt at all that it was Moriarty I was speaking to, albeit from Seton's mouth. There were certain nuances in his accent and patterns of speech that immediately identified him to me. He has indeed found a way to pierce the veil of death."

"But surely..."

I was given no time to continue, as Holmes spoke over me, as if to himself.

"Trust me Watson, he has a bigger plan than just ruining you and I. We are merely a diversion, a way to keep Scotland Yard looking elsewhere while he puts his machinations into action."

I asked Holmes to halt for a while and we sat by the side of the track where we had been walking. I rolled fresh cigarettes and we smoked as Holmes continued.

"It is not power he wants, Watson. With Moriarty it was never the power, despite the fact that he could use his position in the Lords to many purposes. No, his criminal tendencies will out, even now. I suspect he has something big in mind, something that his new situation makes him uniquely qualified for. I just have not hit on the heart of the matter yet. But I will Watson... I will."

When we set off again he let me in on the next part of the plan.

"We must return to London," he said. "And begin a surveillance on his Lordship. That is our only recourse now – foil his plan and we may be able to force a confrontation that will unmask the whole affair. We can only hope that Seton's actions while in London last night will work in our favor."

I admit I was still skeptical of the whole affair. I could not bring myself to believe in the transfer of personality in such an esoteric fashion as had supposedly been shown to us. But it seemed that Holmes intended to proceed as if it were fact, and I decided that I must play along, and see the thing through to the conclusion. After all, I did not have many other options, as handing myself in at that point would have served no purpose at all now that we had burned our bridges with Lestrade.

««« — »»»

We spent two more days getting as far as Edinburgh thanks to a lot of walking on country pathways and some fortuitous carts of produce driven by farmers that happened to be going in our direction. There was also rather too much dodging through hedgerows and slogging through muddy fields to avoid being seen, so much so that I'm afraid our clothing took rather a beating in the process. By the time we arrived in the capital we were once more threadbare, mud-strewn and bedraggled.

Holmes however had an answer for that, and as he had done in Glasgow, he led me straight to a bar. This one was in the Grassmarket in the shadow of the Castle, and reaching it needed a degree of stealth and the luck of arriving during some heavy rain that kept the streets quiet. I felt somewhat like a drowned rat however when he led me into the bar's doorway. He rapped three times and we were allowed entry into an empty bar.

Holmes was greeted like an old friend by the barkeep. Over a bowl of very welcome hot soup and more ale we discovered that we had become quite a pair of notorious celebrities. News of our escapade in Comrie, and Lestrade's humiliation in being tied up, had reached the press. Holmes suspected Seton's hand in that matter as there was also a tale being told of our escape via a boat to Skye and then heading for France. I supposed that particular tale appealed to Seton's sense of fun, being a mirror of Bonnie Prince Charlie's own flight from the country. There was also news that Lord Crawford had recanted his statement of our guilt, then just as suddenly changed his mind again. My skepticism regarding what had happened in the Keep was slowly being chipped away.

We stayed in that bar for three days, during which Holmes made plans for our return to London and I caught up with some much-needed sleep in a room upstairs. When not abed I drank more ale and smoked more cigarettes than were good for me. My only contact with the greater world outside was through the newspapers. We made the front page of *The Scotsman* which reported our escape from Skye as if it were a fact, complete with an eyewitness report from a local fisherman who had *seen* us getting aboard a boat in the dead of night. There was a quote from Lestrade, who was also in Skye, who said he would be *"pursuing Holmes across the continent if that is what it took to bring him to justice."* An accompanying satirical cartoon showing two rather fine drawings of Lord Crawford arguing with each other about our guilt and innocence. I was starting to wonder just how close to the truth that might be.

I was near to climbing the walls with boredom and frustration by the time Holmes announced he was ready to start the journey south. The announcement came on his return from a trip into the New Town. He did not tell me where he had been, but he waved a sheaf of papers at me.

"Our job is much tougher than we originally thought Watson." He took a cigarette from me and joined me by the fire before continuing. "I have been researching the Seton family and have found an alarming fact. There exists, in London of all places, a whole scion of the family descended directly from Angus himself. I missed it earlier because I was focusing on Lords and minor dignitaries, but this branch of the family has its roots firmly in the working class. A bastard son of Angus' went to Ireland in the late Sixteenth Century – and it is from him that the line descends. I have found that there are at least twenty men in the East End that can claim direct descent. And if I can find them, then so can Moriarty."

"But why would he?" I asked. "What use would he have of any of them when he could have a Lord of the realm or, if you believe in it, the body of the immortal head of the clan?"

Holmes looked grave.

"It is merely one more thing we have to consider. I have made contact with Mycroft," he said. "It seems that our good Lord Crawford is not a well man and has been confined to his rooms. Mycroft says that the man is not happy at the prospect, whether it is when he is employing a Scottish accent or not. Mycroft also says that there is now more than enough doubt about the so-called murder that, if it ever came to trial, the case would be dismissed immediately."

"Then we are free to return?"

Holmes shook his head.

"Mycroft is as yet unwilling to admit to the possibility that Crawford is, at least some of the time, actually Moriarty. Until I can *prove* that fact to his satisfaction he will not call Scotland Yard off the scent. No, we must return incognito if we are to have any success at all in clearing our names.

"I'm afraid more mummery is called for Watson," he said. "I would have liked to return to town openly, but I'm afraid that there has been too much excitement and noise around the case for that to be possible. What say you? Shall we return to our earlier personas... or would you entertain the thought of something rather more exotic?"

«««—»»»

SHERLOCK HOLMES: REVENANT

I made the trip to London in the guise of an eighty-year-old Churchman; slightly deaf and mostly cantankerous. It was a role I found remarkably easy to play given my growing dissatisfaction with this case. Holmes did not help my mood by being relentlessly cheerful all the way South, as if delighted to be returning to familiarity.

The only thing that stopped my mood from descending completely into the depths was the fact that the journey went smoothly. No one took much notice of us, and even the few policemen we saw seemed to have lost interest in looking for the escaped murderers. Holmes judged that there was now a common belief that we had fled to the continent and by the time we left York behind I was starting to believe him.

I had expected more policemen to be waiting at Euston on our arrival back in the city but there was only a single officer on the concourse, and he paid us no heed whatsoever. This only seemed to embolden Holmes. He headed straight for Baker Street.

He was not so indiscreet as to enter through the front entrance but went round to the rear and opened the scullery door. He almost received a blow on his head for his trouble, for Mrs. Hudson was in the room and, taking him for an intruder, aimed a skillet at his head. Fortunately he managed to duck in time, but he had to remove his false whiskers before she recognized us and put the pan down.

If she was happy to see us she did not show it at first, berating us, firstly for our stupidity for being caught in the trap and, secondly, for not letting her know that we were safe and not in fact absconded to the continent. Immediately after that she burst into tears and only a cup of strong tea revived her to something like her former efficient self. We were forcibly told to sit at her kitchen table. We told her our tale while she moved around us preparing a meal.

"I'll soon have you back to normal," she said, as if we were somehow starved and wasted. Indeed it seemed she would attempt to do it all at once as she plied us with scones, cream, jam and several cups of her special strong tea. Holmes let me do most of the talking, only interjecting where he thought I had made an error or had mis-remembered something. Mrs. Hudson listened intently, then surprised us.

"I've heard of him," she said. "He was always known as wee auld man Seton. There are plenty of stories told in Scotland about his exploits over the years. My grandmother, God rest her soul, even swore to us that she met him in Edinburgh once back in the '40s. She said he was a prodigious liar, but very charming in his own way."

Having that connection in her own personal history meant that the rest of my tale did not sound outlandish to her in the slightest, and where I had been expecting disbelief I got instead a calm acceptance. I finished with a question as to where we went from here.

"Mister Holmes will find a way," she said with a quiet confidence I did not quite share. And she proved herself quite adept at subterfuge when she installed thick curtains in the main rooms of our apartment. Once these were closed she was confident that no light, and therefore no sign of our presence, would show from the outside.

So it was we were able to achieve some relaxation amid all the comforts of home. But if I had expected to be allowed to enjoy an evening at ease Holmes soon put me right when it came round to nightfall.

"I intend to make a foray to the East End in search of information about the Seton offshoots. We must ascertain whether Moriarty is aware of them or indeed whether they have not already fallen under his malign influence. Are you game?"

"Now?" I said, and Holmes must have heard the reluctance in my voice. He laughed.

"Stay here then old friend, with your warm fire and your pipe and slippers. I shall report on my adventures on my return."

Of course he knew I would rise to the taunting. Ten minutes later I was at his side as we left the apartment and made for the scullery door.

«««—»»»

Our only attempt to hide our appearance was in the wearing of long overcoats and hats with wide brims pulled low over our brows. We scarcely needed to have made the effort, as it was a damp night with the air full of fog and drizzle, and anyone out on the streets was more intent on hurrying home against the weather than in looking too closely at us.

Which was just as well as Holmes' burst of confidence did not stretch far enough to consider taking a carriage. I resigned myself to the prospect of a long, wet, walk. I became rather glad of the overcoat and hat over the next hour as we strode through mostly quiet streets headed for Whitechapel. We took a northerly route to keep away from the busier streets near the city center and the only time we met with any great density of people was when we skirted the Angel Islington before turning south and east.

"What are we hoping to find?" I asked Holmes as we approached the Liverpool Street area. At first I was not sure he would answer. He had been quiet for most of the walk so far, not so much taciturn as lost in contemplation. In anyone else it might be thought rudeness but I had become accustomed to long silences over the years. In fact, on some occasions I have even been known to welcome them. On this particular night, Holmes decided to reply.

"I'm looking for a clue," he said. "A means by which we might start to make some headway against the obstacles Moriarty has so successfully put in our path. I hope to find some of the Seton offshoots, MacAllan as they are now known, and question them, or at least discover whether there have been any recent unusual bouts of *sleeping sickness* in the family."

And at that he went quiet again, walking faster now as we approached our target.

Our first port of call was a pawnbroker's shop on a corner opposite the old East India Company warehouse at Devonshire Square.

It was a veritable Aladdin's cave, containing more jewelry than I had seen outside Bond Street, row after row of brass and stringed musical instruments and, behind a heavy mahogany counter, a back chamber that seemed to be full of rich furs and overcoats.

Holmes was obviously known to the proprietor, and was greeted warmly.

"Long time no see Mr. Holmes," the small man said. He could have been any age from sixty to ninety years old, stooped and bent so much that he needed the use of a cane to keep him upright. He wheezed when he spoke, like a deflating rugger ball, but his eyes were clear and bright, and I suspected there was not much that got past him.

Holmes spent some time in pleasantries before asking about the whereabouts of any members of the MacAllan family. The old man sucked at his teeth and waved his free hand in a seesaw manner.

"Here and there Mr. Holmes, here and there if you catch my drift?"

Fortunately Holmes understood the man's intent more clearly than I did. Money changed hands and we were given directions to a public bar that I vaguely knew near the Effingham Theatre.

"But beware Mr. Holmes," the pawnbroker said. "They like a drink those lads, and when they're in their cups they also like to fight."

Holmes thanked the man and we went back out into the night. The rain was heavier now, and we hurried along the narrow cobbled streets to the bar, our feet splashing in newly formed puddles.

Holmes stopped outside the bar door. It was apparent that the place was busy, the sound of raucous banter seeping through the thick external door.

"And now we must take a risk Watson," he said. "There will be people inside who know us, and they are not the kind to look the other way if they think the police might pay for their information. We may end up paying dearly for anything we learn. But I believe this is our only course of action. Are you with me?"

"Always old chap," I replied with more bravado than I felt at that moment. "Lead on."

The bar was another huge barn full of mirrors, mahogany and chandeliers, much like the Horseshoe Bar in Glasgow, but on a far grander scale. I had rarely seen a more opulent establishment, even in the palaces of the Raj. It was also full of people seeming intent on getting inebriated as fast as they were able. Street girls worked the room and smartly dressed men from the City mingled with market workers and railwaymen still grimy from their day's labour. Half a dozen bar staff were being kept busy supplying a constant flow of ale and gin, and a space around a card table was the only quiet area in the whole place.

When we entered several people looked our way, but

no one looked twice and Holmes seemed satisfied it was safe to stay, at least for a while.

"I'll go and ask some questions Watson, you keep an eye open for anyone paying too much attention to either yourself or to me."

I retired to the bar, ordered a jug of ale, lit a pipe and watched Holmes as he made his way around the patrons; a tap on the shoulder here, a whispered question there. All of his moves were so subtle that no one took offence and no one noticed that he was slowly but surely homing in on a target.

His attentions soon focussed on three men in particular. All three looked skittish, their eyes straying anywhere but on Holmes' face as he sat at their table, even after he had ordered a fresh round of drinks brought to them. Holmes did not give them time to think, bombarding first one then another with questions. It took around an hour during which time I made some inroads into the ale. The barman was on the verge of pouring me a refill when Holmes rose and came back to my side.

"Well," he said. "We have a story, although I am not yet sure what to make of it. But first, let us take our leave. Too many people have seen us already. I feel as if we are *watched* too closely."

We left the bar. The door shut behind us – and at the same moment I heard a *pop* and a chunk of wood flew. We were under fire again.

«««—»»»

Without pause Holmes was off and running even as I understood what was happening. As he had at King's Cross he made straight for where he guessed the gunman to be. I held my place, just long enough to hear the next *pop* and see a shadow move in the darkness near the entrance to the Effingham Theatre. I thought of calling out, but I saw that Holmes had also spotted the movement and was headed that way at full tilt. Another shot *pinged* off the cobbles near my left foot then I too was running after Holmes.

He reached the theatre some ten yards ahead of me and by the time I too reached the entrance he had already gone inside. I cursed when I reached for my pocket and remembered that I had left a revolver behind in Baker Street. I padded inside as quietly as I could manage, trying to keep to the shadows and not allow my outline to be silhouetted in the doorway. No one shot me.

The theatre foyer lay in deep darkness and I was forced to stand still for long seconds to let my eyes adjust. The business had gone into liquidation some months before, which would explain the slight smell of mildew and the sound of water dripping from my left. The place was obviously already falling into disrepair. I wondered if any of the light fittings actually worked, but that was a moot point as I was not about to try to find out.

"Holmes?" I said in a stage whisper, then immediately regretted it as a *pop* followed straight away and glass broke in a mirror just behind me. I had enough sense about me to move to one side and keep quiet. Silence descended again.

I was feeling exposed, stuck too far into the open in the foyer. I started to shuffle sideward with my arm outstretched, hoping to reach a wall. Instead my hand found something cold and damp and I almost cried out, thinking it was our attacker, but some more investigation proved it to be a heavy velvet curtain that covered an entrance into the theatre proper. When I carefully pulled it aside I immediately felt a cooler breeze on my cheek, and I heard the sound of footsteps on wooden boards.

There was another unmistakable *pop,* a scuffle of feet and a cry of pain. My heart sank, for I thought for sure that Holmes had been hit. But it was my friend's voice that came next through the dark.

"Get down here quickly Watson. I have him."

I followed the sound of his voice, feeling my way down one of the gangways between the rows of seats. As I got closer to the source of the noises I realized I was starting to make out shapes in the darkness, and after several seconds I could make out the stage ahead of me. Holmes knelt, holding down a prone figure on the floor. The other thing I noticed as I got closer was the sound of sobbing, low and soft like a child who was trying to be brave and hold it in.

"Give me a hand here Watson," Holmes said. "I fear I have broken his arm."

Holmes' *victim* proved to be a youth, barely out of his teens by the look of him and dressed in the cheap woolens and heavy work-boots typical of a local market worker. He had his eyes screwed up in pain and his arm had indeed been broken; white bone showed through a tear in the skin just above the wrist. It was also obvious that this lad was the gunman – the weapon lay on the floor beside him, an air gun, as Holmes had surmised.

"Do you know him?" I asked Holmes.

He shook his head.

"I do not, and he does not resemble anyone who has been mentioned to me tonight. But if he is not a MacAllan then I will eat this hat."

"Jimmy MacAllan, that's me sir," the boy said, grimacing through the pain but suddenly latching onto something familiar in the mention of his name.

"Can you get up lad?" I asked him. "We have to get

you to a hospital and get that break seen to."

He tried to shuffle away from us on his backside, banged his arm on the stage and yelped, like a kicked dog.

"Please, don't hurt me again," he whimpered, his obvious East-End roots showing in his speech. Suddenly I felt almost guilty at how we had treated him. I bent to take him by his good arm.

He looked up, fear in his eyes, then suddenly they went out of focus and his mouth went slack – only for a second or so until he smiled broadly.

"That is enough of that," he said, and this time it was in that clipped voice I had first heard back in Lord Crawford's office, and then again under Seton's Keep in Comrie. Three separate bodies, but it was becoming obvious to me that the voice always came from one source, Moriarty himself.

"I only let the boy speak to show you who is in charge here," he said. He looked up at Holmes. "I would advise you to stay away from this side of town," he said, and winked, "It is not safe... as this boy is about to find out."

"No!" Holmes shouted, but his rage was to prove impotent, for there was nothing either he or I could do about what happened next. The boy's eyes went dead again. He started to thrash, feet pounding a rhythm on the wooden boards of the stage. Spittle frothed and flecked from his lips and blood bubbles showed where he had bitten through his tongue. This I *did* know how to deal with – or so I thought.

"Hold him Holmes, he's having a seizure."

But no amount of holding the lad down was going to save him. I was looking in his face when his eyes filled with blood. His neck muscles strained one last time and his mouth gaped. I thought he might scream, but no sound came. He fell back, head hitting the boards of the stage with a sickening soft thud. I checked to make sure but I already knew there would be no pulse. The lad was dead.

"Come Watson," Holmes said softly, taking me by the arm. "We can do no more here."

I shrugged him away.

"We cannot just leave him lying here," I said. "It's not right."

"There is little *right* about this case old friend," Holmes said. "All we can do is ensure that someone who will look after him finds him first. We shall make an anonymous report to the Yard later. But for now we must go. Moriarty knows we are here – there might be more gunmen where this lad came from."

I allowed him to lead me out into the street, and I followed him at a steady pace as we headed back to Baker Street. All the way the lad's dead blood-filled eyes stared at me in my mind's eye.

((((—))))

It was only once we were back in the apartments and settled by the fire with a snifter and a pipe that Holmes talked about the events of the night.

"We are getting somewhere Watson," he said after getting his own pipe lit. "Moriarty would not warn us off unless it were so. And it is indicative of *something* that he has not informed the police that we are back in London, for if he had, I have no doubt Lestrade would be here already to carry out the promises that were made in Comrie. No... we are getting somewhere."

"Did you learn anything of import in the bar?" I asked.

"It was a tortuous process," he started. "But yes, I was eventually able to tease out a thread of narrative

SHERLOCK HOLMES: REVENANT

from the three men who, in case you had not already surmised, were MacAllans by descent, although rather far removed from the original strain; too far indeed to be under Moriarty's influence directly. But I am getting ahead of myself, in much the same way as the three in the bar tended to. I shall attempt to summarize for you Watson but please, be patient with me, for I had a great deal of information to process, some of it contradictory in nature.

"The MacAllan's tale begins in the early Nineties. Of course it begins much earlier than that, with Seton himself, but we shall skip over that for you already know as much as you need to at the moment about the deeper history. We start in the East End, with a family of itinerant laborers, small time thieves and opportunists. As far as I can gather they are rather a large clan now, but some of them are considered more *influential* than others are, being able to claim direct descent from the *auld country* stock. They are a tight-knit bunch by nature as are many of their type in the East End, and do not take easily to prying questions from strangers. But, sometime in early ninety-one, one such stranger appeared with enough money to loosen tongues. I suspect that man to have been Moriarty himself, these encounters taking place in the months immediately preceding our encounter at the Falls.

"The man was particularly interested in genealogy, and proved able to spend rather large sums of money to be informed of family histories. It was not much later that the family members started to suffer what they call *the sleeping lurgy*. By now you will recognize the symptoms - an unconscious state, the mouthing of words and the memory lapse on awakening. Many of the family were struck in this manner over a period of some weeks.

"But it is what happened next that most concerns us," Holmes said gravely. "In May of that year a number of members of the family walked out of the East End and have not been seen again beyond rumored sightings in the City just these past few months. You see what this means of course?"

And of course I was almost as much in the dark as I had been at the start of his tale before it hit me.

"You think Moriarty is somehow using the bodies of these missing people to travel around town?"

Holmes nodded.

"My fear is that by using them as vehicles he has been able to travel and undertake his nefarious plans, all in complete anonymity. I believe he has been working under my very nose all this time without giving a hint of his presence until now. The mere fact that he chose to set a trap for us at this juncture tells me that his plans must be close to fruition. Coupled with the fact that he made another attempt on us this very night means that we must work fast Watson, for time may be short. Get some sleep tonight, for tomorrow we must seek out the missing MacAllans."

««—»»

Finding the missing men proved to be easier said than done. We spent a most frustrating week clad in a variety of disguises, walking the length and breadth of the East End in search of any mention of the MacAllan family. It was only when our search took us towards Wapping that we started to hear stories. Our first intimation came over lunch in *The Prospect of Whitby*. It was a bar that Holmes and I had previously visited several times on cases, and now I worried that our disguises would not pass muster, but we were mostly ignored as we supped some particularly fine ale. We fell into conversation with two fish merchants at the bar.

I sat in silence and watched Holmes work. I continue to be amazed by his ability to blend seamlessly with the character he is portraying and converse at an equal level with any of London's social strata. After spending quarter of an hour relating a completely fictitious but gripping account of a trip across the Channel in a gale he had the men eating out of his hand. During the next hour we got our first hints of the criminal activities of Sad-Eye Joe MacAllan, active in these parts but only having risen to prominence in recent times. The way the man was described; Irish, fiery and quick-witted, but with a strange tendency to drift into lapses of forgetfulness, had me convinced we were indeed on to something with this line of enquiry.

Holmes obviously thought the same. He subtly but firmly quizzed the men and teased out a thread of criminal actions ranging from petty theft to grand larceny, all of which involved Sad-Eye Joe and a small clan of family members. None of the family was ever seen together, and all seemed to suffer sudden bouts of the *sleeping sickness*. The fishermen had not heard whether Joe was plotting anything in particular.

"But it wouldna' surprise me," the elder of the fishermen said. "When somebody suddenly gets ambitious later in life like that who knows what can happen?"

Neither of the fishermen could say exactly where we might find any of these MacAllans, only that they were usually *around*. But Holmes had a smile on his face when we finally parted company with the men at the bar. We took our ales out onto the small balcony that overlooked the river and lit up smokes. Holmes made sure there was no one in hearing range before speaking.

"My hunch was right Watson. Find this family and

we shall have gone a long way towards uncovering Moriarty's plot."

I knew the signs. Holmes now had but a single focus and, like a terrier with a rat would not let go until the job was done.

For the next three days I followed him around some of the most miserable parts of the city I have ever had the misfortune to visit. We listened to tall tales and eyewitness accounts where the *sleeping sickness* was attributed to witchcraft, poison and even the work of old Hob himself. Holmes filed each tale away in its appropriate compartment in that regimented mind of his and moved on. We followed an inward-tending spiral, deep into the heart of the East End, each night hearing more and more about the exploits, mostly criminal in nature, of Sad-Eye Joe. And each morning, as we tried to gain some rest back in Baker Street, Holmes sat in the chair by the fire, smoking his favorite Meerschaum and staring into space, so still that an observer may have thought that he himself was suffering from the very malady we were investigating.

Finally on the fourth evening we made a breakthrough, learning of an address in Shoreditch that three of the MacAllan family members had been seen entering. We arrived in the area at dusk and spent a long hour watching for any sign of activity, none of which was forthcoming. The building itself was a three-story sandstone dwelling, turned black with smoke and soot. It looked like it may at one time have been a warehouse, as there were indeed many such similar buildings in the area, but this one had been converted into a warren of small apartments, cheap housing for poorly paid workers in the local markets. Most of the windows showed no light at all. A single candle flickered on the second floor, but no shadows moved in the room beyond the whole time we were there. Finally Holmes could contain himself any longer.

"Come Watson," he said. "Let us see if tonight is the night we can force him into a confrontation."

I followed him across the street to the doorway. He rapped hard on the door. There was no reply, no sign of movement at all from inside. I made to turn away, but Holmes had other ideas. He turned the handle and put his shoulder to the door. It gave way before him with a loud crack that echoed around the street. I had a quick look round before following Holmes inside; no one seemed to be paying us any attention, and no one shot at me, which I took as a good sign.

Holmes hushed me to be quiet as soon as we entered a long narrow hallway. Unlike the hallway in Seton's Keep in Comrie, this place felt somehow *alive*. The hairs at the nape of my neck rose and I was immediately on the defensive. The atmosphere was stifling; hot and sultry, reminding me strangely of monsoon season in Northern India. Some light found its way in from the street outside, but further inside the dwelling everything was dark and quiet. I was immediately reminded of the events in the Effingham Theatre.

"Is this wise old chap?" I whispered. The sibilant sounds echoed around us, whistling like wind under an ill-fitting door. Holmes hushed me to be silent once more. We padded softly through a series of empty rooms on the ground floor. There was some evidence of recent occupation, but no one had either lit a fire or prepared food there for several days at least. I was starting to think we were on a fool's errand as we climbed the stairs to the first floor.

It was darker here, and the shadows seemed to run around the rooms without any discernable light source to drive them. Or maybe it was just my imagination;

this case had certainly awoken a superstitious corner of my mind I had thought left behind in childhood. When we reached a door and heard heavy breathing coming from beyond, the scared boy I had been did not seem very far away at all.

Holmes had no such qualms. He moved quietly into the room and was soon lost from sight in the dark. Several seconds passed, with no change in the timbre or intensity of the breathing. It sounded like a small group of people, all of them asleep. Even before Holmes called me inside with a stage whisper I knew what I was going to encounter.

Chapter Five

It was only a small room, some ten feet square, but somehow twelve people had managed to find space to sleep in swaddled bundles on the floor, so closely packed that I had to carefully pick my way between them.

Of course I say *sleeping*, but these prone figures proved, to a man, to be in the same almost cataleptic state I was coming to recognize, with all of the same symptoms save one. There was no mouth movement apparent, no attempts at forming words. They just lay there, eyes open, staring vacantly into space. The air felt heavier here, stale food mixed with body odor and the rank acrid stench of clothes worn far too long without washing. I had to cover my mouth with a handkerchief when kneeling to inspect the bodies; that is how I thought of them, for any semblance of personality was completely absent. They were all of them male, with ages ranging from the late teens through to forty at a guess, but there was no sign of the one we had heard described as Sad-Eye Joe.

After a few minutes Holmes motioned that we should leave the room. I was glad to agree. We went out onto the upstairs landing where the air was less foul.

"This cannot be, Holmes," I said, keeping my voice low. "Surely even Moriarty can only control one other man at a time?"

Holmes looked grave.

"There is much about this case that goes against sense Watson," he said. "But I fear this is even worse than I imagined. I think that these poor wretches here are completely lost; their essence, their souls if you like, having moved on, or been forced on, leaving only the husks behind for the puppeteer to play with at his whim."

It took me several seconds to come to terms with what Holmes had said, so far was it from my normal frame of reference as a medical practitioner.

"If that is true, then it is monstrous," I said, and I am afraid that, in my anger, I allowed my voice to rise far beyond the whispers we had been conversing in. A loud moan answered me from the dark room.

Holmes took me by the arm and led me further from the doorway.

"We must keep our presence here quiet," he said softly. "If Moriarty knows we have been here then the game is up. But on the other hand, if we can observe, and follow these poor souls about any business he might have them do, then we can crack this case and bring it to resolution."

The very thought appalled me, and I would have told Holmes so in no uncertain manner, but he was already making his way back downstairs and I was loath to spend more time than was necessary standing alone there in the dark. I followed, taking care to tread lightly, listening at every step for any sign that someone might wake. But I reached the front door with no further mishap.

Holmes was on the doorstep waiting.

"We shall need to work in shifts," he said. "I cannot trust this to anyone else outside you and I. We shall find a room overlooking this spot, keep watch for anyone entering, and follow anyone that leaves.

Agreed?"

"I am more inclined to call in the authorities," I said. "We could after all be dealing with some disease with which I am not familiar?"

Holmes snorted impatiently.

"Rubbish, Watson, and you know it. You have seen enough already to know exactly who is behind this. Will you help me catch him, or must I do this alone?"

Of course, when he put it like that, I could not refuse him.

That same evening we took a room opposite the building, making sure we got a spot where we could watch the comings and goings without being observed ourselves.

It was to be a longer vigil than either of us had imagined.

«««—»»»

By the end of the second day boredom had set in. We took turns sleeping in the saggy bed that dominated one whole side of the room while the other sat by the window and watched for any sign of activity. Between us we got through a prodigious amount of tobacco, and Mrs. Hudson had made three trips already to deliver hampers of food to sustain us. Still, time dragged somewhat, more so when either of us was asleep, or when the black mood took Holmes and he went quiet. As an old soldier I was used to long periods of inactivity between bursts of action, but the tedium of it got to Holmes and eventually he started to fret.

"I may have misjudged the situation, Watson," he said for maybe the fourth time in as many hours. "We should be out looking for Sad-Eye Joe, not cooped up in here watching over the half-dead."

I will admit there had been times over the last few

hours where I would have agreed with him wholeheartedly, but in my mind's eye I kept seeing the dead lad on the stage in the Effingham. I was not yet ready to abandon these others to a similar fate if it could be avoided.

It was almost dark again but we had decided not to show any light from our room in case our presence was noted. So it came to be that I was sitting in the dark on the corner of the bed, smoking yet another pipe of tobacco. I looked up when Holmes pulled the thin curtain aside to better see down into the street. I moved to his side and stared down. There was just enough light from the recently lit gas lamps to see what was happening below. Someone had just come out of the house across the road, a stooped figure heavily wrapped in several layers of clothes. A makeshift hood had been pulled over the head, obscuring the face, but from the general build I surmised this to be one of the younger men I had examined in the room. Quite how they survived for so long in that state I was completely unable to comprehend, and I had never expected to see any of them alive again, never mind out on the street and walking around.

"Finally," Holmes said. "Some action. Stay here, Watson. I will follow our man. You must watch in case anything else happens. I will return as quickly as I can."

With that I was left alone in the dark room with only my pipe for company.

The night passed slowly, made even more so by Holmes' absence. I had to open the window and let some fresh air in for the stuffy heat threatened to send me asleep. Even then I was hard pushed to keep my eyes open. As the night wore on and there was no activity forthcoming I found my mind wandering, turning over aspects of the case. I always returned to that single image I could not seem to let go, of the dead lad in the theatre, and the blood-filled eyes staring up at me.

Sometime later I came awake with a start, immediately annoyed that I had let myself down; let Holmes down. And on looking into the street I saw that I had roused myself just in time. A swaddled figure crossed the street from somewhere below me and went into the building opposite. At first I thought it was Holmes himself, for there was something about the bearing that I recognized, but this was a stockier, shorter man than my friend.

I wondered whether it was another member of the MacAllan clan, possibly even one flushed out by whatever Holmes was up to. But this newcomer's intent was much more sinister, and rapidly became clear when, only seconds after he entered the building, one of the upstairs windows smashed sending a tinkle of glass down to the cobbles. Red and yellow flames immediately showed, lapping around the window frame.

Someone intended to burn the unconscious men.

««—»»

I could not sit idly by and watch mass murder be committed under my nose. I had my revolver in hand as I sped downstairs and across to the building opposite. Flames now rose from three of the windows above and a rising clamor grew in the street as the fire was spotted. I knew it would not be long before action was taken, for a fear of a conflagration in the narrow streets was ever present and something the locals were most vigilant in preventing. But they would not be able to respond fast enough to save the sleeping men. Without a pause for thought I ran into the building.

The hallway beyond was lit in flickering red from the

stairwell and I could see immediately that it was going to be almost impossible for me to reach the room where the men slept.

"Fire!" I called at the top of my lungs. There were answering calls from outside, but inside the building there was only the crackle and roar as fire took ever greater hold. I went to the foot of the stairs and was about to head up in an attempt to at least save one man if I could when I was met by a figure coming down. He was no more than a silhouette backed by flame. The upstairs area was now fully aflame, and black smoke billowed overhead, further obscuring my view. I felt smoke tickle in my throat and nasal passages. Time was getting short.

"Thank Heavens, are there any others with you?" I said, before I remembered the man I had seen coming in.

"I doubt that Heaven has anything to do with it," a voice said. It was a soft Scottish accent. The figure turned sideways, his profile suddenly outlined against the fire and smoke. It could only be one man... Lord Crawford. I was so astonished that I neglected to defend myself as he raised a hand, and I saw the stick he wielded too late. A sharp blow to the head sent me down to blackness.

«««—»»»

Coming back out of the darkness proved to be hard work, like struggling uphill into a high wind. It felt like a drummer pounded a beat in my ear and my eyes were heavy and tired. I heard the crackle of fire and jerked myself awake.

To my astonishment I came to sitting at the fireside in the apartment in Baker Street. Holmes sat opposite, out of disguise and clad in evening dress. He raised an eyebrow as I sat up and groaned.

"Good to see you are back in the land of the living old friend," he said.

I tasted smoke at my lips and smelled it on my clothes.

"What happened?" I asked.

He laughed, but there was little humor there.

"I was rather hoping you could tell me. Mrs. Hudson found you in the scullery, slouched in a chair. You gave her rather a shock, and you're lucky she held back from using the skillet on you."

It all came back to me in a flash.

"It was Crawford," I said. "The blaggard hit me. Though how I got to be back here I do not know."

Holmes raised an eyebrow again.

"It seems we both have stories to tell of this night's work," he said. "But first, I suggest you get yourself out of that disguise and into some clean clothes. I'll get Mrs. Hudson to bring up an early breakfast and we can swap stories."

I made my way to the bathroom and spent some time recovering my composure. My eyes kept getting drawn to a fresh bruise and lump on my left brow. It was tender to the touch and throbbed constantly, but the pain was bearable, and would soon be made less so with liberal consumption of some brandy.

I rejoined Holmes in the sitting room already feeling somewhat refreshed. He had been as good as his word and there was a plate of poached eggs and toast waiting for me that I took to with some gusto. Then, over brandy and a pipe we brought each other up to date.

In truth it did not take me long to tell my side of the tale, for I remembered nothing I have not already related here, having no memory at all of any journey from Shoreditch to Baker Street. But Holmes listened to it all most intently.

He only asked one question, and that was when I finished.

"It was Crawford, and he spoke with a Scots accent?" Holmes asked.

I nodded.

"It could be no other."

I knew from Holmes' general demeanor that I had just missed something, something important, but slightly befuddled as I was what with a blow to the head and several stiff drinks inside me, I failed to see it for myself. But Holmes' thin smile told me that he was onto something. I poured myself a less generous drink, got a fresh pipe going and sat back to hear his account to the night's adventures.

«««—»»»

"I shall start by filling in some of your blank spots Watson," he said, getting a pipe of his own lit. "I arrived back in Shoreditch to find the building completely aflame. I was told that everyone inside had perished, and when I did not find you in the room we had taken I feared the worst. Deducing that, if you were unharmed, you would be making your way back here, I returned with some haste only to find Mrs. Hudson in the scullery trying to wake you. Between her and myself we managed to get you up here by the fire... and the rest you know."

It was still too sketchy and unsatisfying to me. I felt like part of my life had been stolen. And with that thought came another.

"I say Holmes," I said, cold fear suddenly gripping me. "You don't think I fell with that bally *sleeping sickness* do you? Surely Moriarty has not been using *me* as a puppet?"

Holmes shook his head.

"Not unless you have Seton ancestry of which you are completely unaware. Besides, that lump on your head tells me that you were *really* out for the count. No. There is another mystery here, one I think I may now have an answer for. But that is for later. For now, let us go back to when I left you earlier in the evening. The particulars of my story may illuminate some of the blank spots in yours."

He stared into the fire for long seconds collecting his thoughts then started the story proper.

"I arrived outside just as my quarry turned the corner at the end of the street. By the time I reached the corner he was already some way ahead and walking quite rapidly so that I had to hurry to keep him in view. The streets were rather empty so I found I had to stay some way back to prevent being spotted, but after a while I noticed that he seemed to be moving with singular purpose, looking neither to one side or the other. I felt confident enough to move up closer and we went that way for quite some time, with my quarry some fifty yards or so ahead of me.

"After a while I began to get some sense of where we were going. We headed south on the approaches to Liverpool Street Station and down the warren of streets between Moorgate and the Bank. I thought we might be headed for the Bank itself but he took a turn east and we made our way along just north of St. Paul's. He finally reached his destination; a large hole in the ground which denoted the workings for the new Central railway system. You may remember that one of the things Seton found on his Lordship's desk was a ledger detailing its construction?

"My quarry descended into the workings having passed a night guard with no more than a wave of his hand but when I attempted the same I was stopped and asked for identification. I had to part with a five-pound note before I was allowed access and not only did I lose track of my quarry for a while, I fear I also roused the suspicion of the night guard and I do believe he might have recognized me. But I could not spare any worry on that matter, for I needed to catch the man I had followed here. I went down into the new tunnel.

"I was amazed at how far the work has progressed down there. There is a defined tunnel and track system already in place, well lit at regular intervals with electric lights. By those lights I was able to see my man some a hundred yards further on. I followed as swiftly as I was able but on coming to a bend in the track I found no sight of him ahead. I knew I had not passed him, so there was only one option – he had gone through some kind of concealed entrance.

"I found it seconds later, a cunningly wrought panel that only opened on the correct application of pressure. I slid inside and into another tunnel, one far less well finished than before, and one that was much narrower. It was also obviously still under construction for I heard the distinctive sound of pick on stone from further on inside. It was darker here and I was once again able to close in on the man. And by doing so I was able to witness the most remarkable thing. My quarry was still walking in a very stilted manner, almost as if being led by a set of strings. He walked the length of the corridor to where a much larger man, one I immediately recognized as our long-sought Sad-Eye Joe, toiled hard with a pick-axe to lengthen the tunnel further. When the two men were less than three feet apart the larger man put the pick down and, in a move you would now recognize Watson, fell into the *sleeping* posture. The new man, much less stilted now, lifted up the pick and started to dig.

"I believed I had discovered Moriarty's purpose in using the men; he has been using them to dig, and from the angle and depth of the tunnel itself it was going in a straight line to his goal – the vaults of the Bank of England."

««—»»

Holmes gave me some time to digest this information before continuing.

"I say I *believed* I had discovered his purpose, but a closer inspection of the work in progress soon disabused me of that notion. There was a rough and ready approach in evidence and the whole effort seemed somewhat lackadaisical and lacking in planning; not something we would normally associate with Moriarty. It was almost as if it was a stage set. And when I saw the small barrels lined against the walls I got a further clue as to what was on the agenda here – the barrels were full of black powder, enough to blow a rather large hole in that part of London."

I stopped Holmes at this point.

"But that is not a plan I would attribute to Moriarty either," I said. "What profit is there in such an act for him?"

Holmes smiled thinly.

"Precisely Watson. But you have failed to see the whole picture. I will come to that anon. Let me return to that rough-hewn chamber and the MacAllans.

"I stayed there for perhaps half an hour while the man made some half-hearted attempts at enlarging the chamber before I realized I had learned all I could at this visit. My choices were to stay, or to return to Shoreditch and rejoin you in the watch.

"I backed out of the chamber silently, and made my

way back to the hole by which I had entered and left. This time the guard did not even acknowledge my existence.

"And so here we are, back where I began. But I have several points we have not yet considered. Firstly, there is the matter of your encounter with Lord Crawford. Or rather, someone *using* Lord Crawford. I have been thinking on the timing of events, and I can assure you Watson that the presence we know as Moriarty was most definitely employed with a pickaxe at the time. Whoever you met, it was not Moriarty. And we only know of one other capable of such a thing – it must have been Seton himself. He probably knew that you would want to interfere, which will be why he knocked you out, then looked after you by bringing you here."

I must admit that took me aback somewhat.

"But he murdered all those men. They were his kin."

"I doubt he sees it as murder. I think you'll find that, like me, he believes the men's essence to be long gone. He may well see the act as doing a last service for the poor unfortunates to avoid Moriarty *desecrating* them further."

I still could not agree. As a doctor I had seen people come out of catalepsy none the worse for the experience. If there was a chance of life, the human mind found a way to take it. But yet again I was finding my view of how things were *meant* to work was being challenged, and I had to change my view of things – an occurrence that was becoming all too common these past weeks. I would have pointed that out to Holmes there and then but a knock at the downstairs door interrupted us.

"That will be our carriage," Holmes said, as if he had been expecting it. "I have asked for a meeting with Mycroft. Rather than repeat myself further I will save my conclusions until then. And bring your revolver Watson. We may have need of it before this thing is done."

Minutes later we were once more on our way to the Houses of Parliament. Holmes seemed energized, ready for action, but for myself I went with a degree of trepidation, for our last such visit had not ended well for us at all.

«««—»»»

As it transpired I had worried unduly. The carriage took us to the Member's entrance and deposited us as close to the door as he could such that we were able to disembark with no one seeing us. Mycroft himself was waiting and without speaking he led us through a warren of corridors to a small basement room. It was only when we were inside with the door closed behind us that he seemed to relax.

"I did as you asked in the telegram," he said, pouring three glasses of claret and passing them out. "Crawford did indeed manage to get out last night, but he came back of his own accord; slightly confused I must admit. And I have put a watch on the railway workings at Bank. But for pity's sake Holmes, tell me what's going on here."

Holmes sipped at his claret, savoring the moment before starting. He related much the same tale he had told me back in Baker Street before reaching the point where he had stopped previously.

"As I was about to tell Watson earlier," he said. "I believe the whole setup in the railway tunnel to be another trap, an elaborate ruse designed purely to once again throw us off the scent. And, like the earlier trap, it will have a secondary purpose. I have not yet fully determined what that might be yet, but it will have

115

something to do with both the *Irish Problem* and the Fenchurch Street railway line, mark my words."

At that Mycroft went quite pale.

"How did you know about that Holmes? That is a matter of the *utmost* secrecy."

"And this *utmost secret*," Holmes said, somewhat sarcastically. "Did Lord Crawford have access to it?"

If anything Mycroft went even paler.

"We must go, and quick. The Home Secretary needs to hear this. Pray we have time."

"Time for what?" I asked.

It was Holmes who answered.

"I may be wrong, but I do not believe so. The Home Secretary recently put measures in place to deal with suspected acts of terror in the Financial District." He looked at Mycroft, who nodded in confirmation. "And I do believe one of those is the removal of Britain's bullion reserves to a safe place... by means of a special train from Fenchurch Street."

Mycroft did not even bother to reply. We followed him at some haste through more corridors to what was obviously a suite of bedchambers. Mycroft showed no qualms in rapping hard on one of the doors. A somewhat bemused man opened it a few seconds later. The Home Secretary looked much smaller out of his usual rather formal dress and wearing a nightshirt. He looked at the three of us, then addressed Holmes directly.

"Have you come to throw me out of a window too?"

Mycroft looked fit to burst.

"The Fenchurch Street solution. Tell me it has not been implemented."

The man to his credit took it in his stride.

"Why yes. The memo should be on your desk by now. We had a tip off last evening that the Irish were planning an attack and I ordered the bullion moved for safekeeping. It will all be aboard the train by now."

«««—»»»

And of course, we were too late. Mycroft marshaled an impressive range of men on the ground but by the time we arrived at Fenchurch Street – after another bone-rattling carriage trip along the embankment – the troops and police were just milling around looking lost.

The train, and Great Britain's bullion reserves with it, had gone.

Chapter Six

There was a tremendous tumult of course. Mycroft took charge and sent word ahead down the line to stop all trains going through all eastbound stations, and a thorough search was made of the workings in the railway system under Bank. All that was found there was much gunpowder and two dead men, their eyes filled with blood after suffering some kind of seizure.

But after a few hours it was apparent that Moriarty had won. No trace could be found of the train.

It was Holmes who thought to ask the name of the man put in charge of the transport of bullion. It came as no surprise to him to find that it was a certain John MacAllan, a man who lived a quiet life in Battersea but who on closer inspection was found to have family ties to the MacAllans of the East-End.

As dawn approached, we knew that no further purpose would be served by staying around Fenchurch Street, and Holmes was becoming irritable at Mycroft's demands that we stay hidden in the carriage that had brought us here. When Mycroft finally returned Holmes demanded that we be allowed some freedom.

"Surely you have enough evidence by now that I had nothing to do with the murder?"

Mycroft looked like a man in need of a good night's sleep.

"I'll get word to Lestrade to call the dogs off," he said. "We have more pressing problems at hand. I trust I can

SHERLOCK HOLMES: REVENANT

count on your help?"

Both Holmes and I were in agreement with that. But Holmes' next request seemed like a strange one to me.

"Would it be possible to have a meeting with Lord Crawford?" he said. "As soon as it can be arranged?"

Mycroft waved a hand in assent. We left Fenchurch Street and the carriage took us back to Parliament.

«««—»»»

At first I thought our return trip had been in vain. Lord Crawford had once more fallen into the now familiar unconscious state. The man had been placed sitting up in an armchair in what I took to be a private room where Members could have a moment's peace. There were several armchairs and small tables arranged in a semi-circle around a tall fireplace.

I checked on Crawford. As I got closer I smelled smoke on his clothes. Holmes saw my reaction.

"Yes. There is no doubt it was this man, or rather this body, that you met in Shoreditch."

Mycroft was still having trouble getting to grips with this part of our story. After he arranged some breakfast for us I told him my tale of the happenings of the night before. The breakfast arrived during my telling and I interspersed my story with mouthfuls of toast and some strong sweet tea. Mycroft in the meantime kept looking over at Crawford.

"Sorry," Mycroft said when I finished. "Despite all you have told me, I still cannot bring myself to believe in this mumbo-jumbo."

At that very instant Crawford shook himself like a dog, raised his head and smiled.

"Ah. The Three Musketeers," he said. I immediately recognized the clipped English accent, so different from the soft Scots voice I had heard in Shoreditch. He sat up in the chair, the smile widening.

"Well Holmes, I think you can now admit that on this occasion I have indeed bested you."

Holmes did not reply, and Mycroft looked too dumbfounded to speak.

"I did not however come to gloat," Moriarty said. "I am finished here, with you, and with this body. Killing two birds with one stone so to speak. Good-bye."

The man's eyes went dead, then he started to thrash, feet pounding a rhythm on the carpet. I was up and across to him almost immediately, but I was far too late. His eyes filled with blood and he slumped in the chair. I checked his pulse just to make sure but there was no doubt about it. The man was as dead as anyone I have ever examined.

So you can imagine my surprise when just seconds later the body shook again, the head come up, and a soft Scots voice spoke.

"Good evening gentleman. I'm sorry if I gave you a scare, but I had to wait until the previous occupant departed."

Mycroft almost fell off his chair.

"Crawford? Is that you?"

"I'm afraid not sir. Lord Crawford has taken his leave. Angus Seton, at your service."

He turned and looked at me.

"I'm right sorry to have hit you last night doctor," he said. "But I did not know how much time I had, and you would have had too many questions."

I felt anger rise in me.

"Not only did you hit me – you killed all those men."

He shook his head, and there was sadness in his voice.

"No doctor. They were dead already. Just like this body here, the spirit has fled, leaving only a shell behind. And I would not desecrate this one so if it were not such an urgent matter."

He turned his attention to Holmes.

"I thought I might find you here or at least be able to get a message to you. I managed to find him. I take it you know about the train?"

Holmes nodded and Seton continued.

"I could only make contact for a few seconds," he said. "But that was long enough. He took several diversions to throw you off the scent and is now on the Eastern Counties Railway tracks, making for Colchester and then for Norwich. He intends to transfer the bullion to a boat. That is as much as I could discover."

"It is enough," Mycroft said. He seemed to have got over his reluctance to believe our story, and left the room in a hurry, no doubt to act on the information.

"And where are you Mr. Seton?" Holmes asked.

The man smiled.

"Nowhere near Norwich," he said. "That was for your brother's benefit. We both know that this must be finished between Moriarty and ourselves, not with any official interference?"

"So where is he really?" Holmes asked without confirming Seton's previous point. He did not have to - I saw the agreement in his face.

"He never left London," Seton replied. "He took the train into a disused tunnel. His idea of a little joke I suppose - he is hiding out in Limehouse, beneath the eastbound viaduct, biding his time. In the morning he intends to take the Rotherhithe tunnel south of the river and thence to Dover, where he has a boat waiting. I suggest you get to the train with all haste before he decides to make a run for it."

Holmes stood.

"Thank you sir. Let us hope that together we can

bring this to a conclusion."

Seton nodded.

"And now, I must leave this poor man's body, entrusting you with the proper care and attention to his funeral. Good-bye, gentlemen. I shall see you soon."

He dropped his head and went still.

When I checked his pulse he was dead.

Again.

«««—»»»

Holmes and I managed to slip out of Parliament while Mycroft was busy elsewhere. It did however seem that he had been as good as his word, for we passed several policemen none of whom so much as looked at us.

We managed to flag down a carriage and were shortly on our way back to the East End, once again suffering a bone-rattling trot along the Embankment.

"We are approaching a conclusion Watson," Holmes said as the carriage turned off towards Monument. "As yet I am not sure how we shall catch Moriarty, or even if such a thing is possible. But we can at least stop him in this latest crime and recover the bullion."

"That certainly must be a priority," I replied. "The fate of the Empire may rest on it."

Holmes almost laughed.

"I leave the fate of empires to Mycroft. Let us be content with catching a thief; albeit a very good one."

I had my own worries to contend with, and while the carriage took us through the warren of streets beyond Monument on the way to the docks I gave voice to the chief of them.

"I am not entirely sure we can trust Seton," I said. "Not after the affair in Shoreditch."

"I agree in part," Holmes said. "The Scotsman clearly has an agenda of his own. But if he meant us harm he has had ample opportunity before now, both in Comrie and in Shoreditch. And he has provided us with clues when we have needed them. We have taken him at his word thus far, and he has not been proved totally false. If this latest lead is true then he will have gone a long way in gaining some trust with me."

As for myself, I was still ambivalent on the matter; still fretting over those swaddled defenseless bodies burning in silence under Seton's hand. I forced it from my mind, a distraction that could be dealt with later. For now Holmes needed me focused and ready for action. The bruise on my head still hurt like billy-ho but the drumbeat throbbing had eased to a manageable level and the weight of the revolver was a reassuring presence in my pocket.

Half an hour later the carriage dropped us off outside Limehouse station. Holmes had us alight on the side opposite the station entrance and took me, by a series of narrow alleyways and passages, under the station itself. We stopped under the high arch of a brick viaduct.

"Quiet now Watson," Holmes said. "If the train is where Seton said it would be, it is just around this next corner. We do not even know what this John MacAllan looks like, so from now on we should treat everyone as a possible suspect. Agreed?"

"Agreed."

I followed him round the corner, revolver in hand.

«««—»»»

There was indeed a train in the tunnel ahead of us, and I was somewhat relieved to see that the engine was not up to steam. There was no driver visible, no one stoking the furnace. We sidled along the side of the carriages into the darkness of the tunnel itself. Still there was no sound, no sign of anyone being present.

"I say Holmes, are you sure we have the right train?"

He did not speak but jumped up into the space between two carriages and pulled aside a canvas tarpaulin that had been tied across the top, moving the material aside just enough so that he could look inside. He turned to me.

"We have the right train Watson, there is no doubt of that."

Even before he finished the sentence there was a *pop*. A bullet tore at Holmes' coat and I did not see whether he had been injured as he jumped down beside me and pulled me into the space between the wheels under the carriage.

"I had hoped to investigate a bit further before being seen," he said. "But it cannot be helped. Let us see if we can outflank this gunman. Keep to the walls, and keep low. I'll go left."

And as quick as that he was gone, running along the side of the track deeper into the tunnel. As soon as he left cover there was another *pop* and this time I was able to locate the source better; the gunman was indeed deeper in the tunnel and would be able to see any movement ahead of him silhouetted against the tunnel entrance. I left my spot under the carriage and leapt for the relative safety of the deeper shadows against the wall. I almost didn't make it; the *pop* of the gun and a whine close to my ear telling me I had been lucky not to be shot.

The bulk of the train obscured any view I might have of Holmes but another *pop* told me that he had broken cover. I used that as cover of my own and moved further into the tunnel. I had to stop after only ten yards, wanting to allow my eyes time to adjust but I was not given time as another *pop* told me that Holmes was still under fire. I headed further into the darkness.

"He's ten yards ahead of you, on the carriage roof," I heard Holmes shout. I sent a shot in that direction, the muzzle flare leaving a yellow afterimage behind my eyes that took long seconds to fade. There was no cry of pain but I heard a scuffle from that direction; Holmes had used my shot as an opportunity to press an attack. And now there *was* a cry of pain, although I didn't know whether it came from Holmes or the gunman. The scuffling continued for a few seconds then was followed by a loud *thud* as bodies fell from the train roof to the tunnel floor.

"I have him Watson," Holmes called, and I moved to his aid as my eyes finally adjusted to the dim light. But again, I was too late. Holmes knelt over another dead body, its eyes filled with blood.

Deeper still in the tunnel someone laughed. When they spoke it was in that clipped English voice I was coming to hate.

"You did not think it would be that easy, did you Holmes? Why not come back here and we can talk about this like civilized men."

At the same time I heard noises from the front of the train; the unmistakable clatter of coal being shoveled into the furnace. Someone was preparing the engine for travelling.

"I mean it Holmes," Moriarty's voice said. "I have someone else here too; a *very* old friend of yours I believe. Come back here and join me and maybe I will let him live."

Holmes started to stand.

"No, Holmes," I said, holding him back. "It is just another trap – don't you see?"

"If it is, it is one I walk into with my eyes open," he said and, pulling away from me, stood. He put out a hand to help me up. "And I would like your company at the end, if you wish to join me?"

"Lay on MacDuff," I said, and let him help me up.

"Just leave the revolver behind, Doctor," Moriarty said from the darkness. "You will not be needing it."

Holmes nodded.

"An end with Moriarty will be between him and I," he said. "Come, bear witness for me."

I left the pistol on the tracks and together we followed Moriarty's voice into the tunnel.

««—»»

We did not have to go far. We walked past four large goods carriages I guessed were the ill-gotten gains. After the second I started to see dim light at the rear of the train showing us to two opulent Pullman carriages hooked behind the cargo. A man stood at the steps between the two carriages. I did not recognize him, but when he spoke the voice was unmistakable.

"Welcome gentlemen. As you can see, I have arranged for us to travel in style. One of the perks of having Lord Crawford make the arrangements."

He showed us inside the rearmost carriage. The interior lived up to the promise of the outside, being a wonder of mahogany, leather and hand-painted mirrors. In feel it reminded me of nothing less than one of the more exclusive gentlemen's clubs, a feeling reinforced by the six armchairs that dominated the center of the space.

Even more astonishing still was the fact that the Scotsman, Seton was sitting in one of the armchairs, cradling a whisky. He had a rueful grin on his face as we entered.

"Greeting gentlemen," he said. "We meet again. I'm afraid I was too hasty and tried an attempt of my own at heroism and saving the day before you arrived. I'm ashamed to say I am not as young as I once was, and our friend here bested me to the extent that I yielded – for now. His whisky is the good stuff though, so I suggest you get some inside of you before he starts talking. It might make the gloating more bearable."

Moriarty laughed. It was only now we were in stronger light that I was able to see that he inhabited a young man's body. He wore the clothes of a clerk, and not a very well paid one at that, with dried ink on his fingers and thin hair already going prematurely bald on top. What *was* left of the hair was a mousy brown with hints of red, and I guessed this must be the aforementioned John MacAllan.

"What is to stop the three of us rushing you, right here," I said.

Moriarty laughed.

"Go ahead, if that is your pleasure. I shall simply *jump* again and leave you with another dead man on your hands. Would you *really* like that doctor? Are you not tired yet of the trail of dead you are leaving behind you?"

"But at least we would be able to retake the train."

Holmes replied this time.

"No Watson. Given the ease with which he performed the last switch, I suspect there are more *available* bodies nearby. Probably in that other Pullman carriage yonder."

Moriarty said nothing. He did not have to. It was not too great a stretch of the imagination for me to imagine the swaddled bodies, crammed together there in the dark, eyes staring but unseeing, just lying there, breathing softly... waiting. I decided then and there that I would not allow him to desecrate more bodies.

At that moment the train gave a lurch and the sound

of the engine starting up rumbled through the carriage.

"Make yourself comfortable gentlemen," Moriarty said. "We have a longish journey ahead of us but, as Mr. Seton has already pointed out, the single malt is particularly fine."

The train started up and, rather than try to keep our balance in the now swaying compartment, we took a chair each while Moriarty served us Scotch. Rarely have I taken part in a more disconcerting tableau, but Holmes seemed to be rather relaxed about the situation so, suspecting he might have a plan he had not yet intimated to me, I decided to play along.

"This time, I believe I will gloat," Moriarty said and laughed. "You have to admit, I have bested you this time, Holmes."

Holmes made him wait, taking his time in filling and lighting a pipe.

"And I suppose you have a cunning plan for our demise?" Holmes finally said.

Moriarty laughed again. He seemed to be enjoying himself immensely.

"Demise? Oh no, Holmes. I have no plans to kill you. I want you to be a witness to the full extent of my victory here today... then I want you to remember it for every hour of every day of what I hope will be a long and miserable life."

The *chug* of the wheels on the rails told me that the train was picking up speed. After several minutes the noise intensified into an echoing roar that made any talk impossible until it abated.

"The Rotherhithe tunnel," Moriarty said to Holmes. "We are now south of the river and on our way to Dover. There we shall transfer the bullion to a boat I have waiting and we shall all make our way to Dieppe. There I shall take my leave of you and Watson. Mister Seton will travel with me, for a while at least. And you will have plenty of time to reflect on this defeat."

Now it was Holmes' turn to laugh.

"I believe it is only a defeat when the game is finally over. This is far from over. Don't you agree Mr. Seton?"

The Scotsman had been sitting quietly all this time but now he seemed to rouse himself.

"Indeed Mister Holmes. We are a ways away from the endgame yet," he said. "Although I have already made a gambit that I believe our adversary has missed." He turned to address Moriarty. "You see, your news that you have spare bodies available to you was not news at all, not to me at least. Before I allowed myself to be *captured*, I spent some time next door. You will never desecrate my kin again; I have seen to that... permanently."

For the first time since our arrival Moriarty's grin slipped a little. Seton's by contrast widened into a smile. Holmes too allowed himself a thin-lipped smile.

"I believe you'll find that Mr. Seton is the winner here," Holmes said. "A fact that I am sure I will be able to live with."

Moriarty produced a small pistol from his jacket pocket.

"You may well have stopped me from using my *spares* as you called them," he said. "But that is of little matter for this body here suits me just fine, for now. Later, Mr. Seton, I shall be taking residency in yours, but that too can wait. Let us all just sit here like civilized men for a time. I have no desire to hurt any of you."

"And yet," Holmes said. "You may have to. For you see, you have already lost. While you were telling me all about your little plan for the bullion, Mr. Seton here was back in Parliament in Lord Crawford's body, telling my brother every detail. Is that not right Mr. Seton?"

From where I sat I saw the wink that Holmes sent to Seton, but it would have been completely hidden from Moriarty's view. Seton was smart enough to do his part.

"Yes indeed Mr. Holmes. And right glad he was of the information too. He was sending people to Dover even as I left."

Moriarty's smile had gone completely now, to be replaced by something that looked very much like rage. As for myself, I was starting to see some method in Holmes' and Seton's plan of attack, and I was not greatly surprised by Seton's next move. He stood and started to walk, somewhat shakily due to the motion of the carriage, towards Moriarty.

"You have repeatedly assured me that your purpose is to take this body of mine," he said. "So I am now going to strangle you. You have nowhere else to go and to stop me you will have to shoot me. I have lived a *long* time, as you know. But even I do not take bullets kindly. So let us have at it, you and I."

Moriarty's smile came back again.

"No closer, or I'll shoot your friend here," he said. The gun shifted, and was now pointed straight at my midriff. But only for a second, as Holmes stepped forward, placing himself directly in the path of any shot.

"I do not believe you will rob yourself of a lifetime of gloating," Holmes said. "But if you must, go ahead and shoot."

Even as Moriarty's finger tightened on the trigger, Seton had moved close enough to bat the pistol aside. A shot, painfully loud in the confines of the cabin, shattered one of the fine mirrors. Seton reached for Moriarty's throat.

"You have forgotten something sir," Moriarty said as Seton's hands gripped him. "There is always somewhere else to go."

Moriarty's eyes rolled up in their sockets. At the same time his body slumped, but then almost immediately straightened.

"I'm sorry Holmes," Seton's voice said, but from the MacAllan man's body. "That was closer than I intended."

Moriarty's voice, that clipped English with a hint of the North, came from Seton's mouth.

"And yet, you have lost, for I am now in occupancy," Moriarty said.

I myself was in a degree of some confusion. It was apparent that the essence of Moriarty was now inside Seton – and Seton had somehow taken residence in the MacAllan body. But I had no time then to reflect on it.

Moriarty reached for the pistol, attempting to grab it from Seton's hand. All of a sudden his body jerked, as if jolted with a seizure.

"You may have occupancy," Seton said and laughed. "But as I told you, I was busy before I came here. You have recently thrown many of my kinsmen from their *homes* to leave them dancing in the shadows... which is where I found them. As their Laird, it would be remiss of me not to provide them with shelter in their time of need. Under the terms of your new lease you will be taking joint tenancy."

Seton's, or rather Moriarty's, body jerked again.

"Say hello to the clan Seton, and their brothers the MacAllans," Seton said. "I am afraid they are rather a noisy bunch. But they are all most eager to make your acquaintance."

Moriarty opened his mouth, but it was a loud Scots voice that replied.

"Thank you kindly Angus," the voice said. "We shall take good care of him. He won't be getting out anytime soon. We have locked the doors and closed the windows so to speak."

That voice went, to be replaced by another, more Irish sounding this time, uttering vile unrepeatable threats against Moriarty. Then a third, in a Scots dialect so thick I barely understood every second word, but the intent was very clear. Moriarty himself resurfaced for a second – just long enough to scream. The body jerked in multiple spasms, throwing it to the floor. Spittle started to fleck at the mouth. I moved to check on him, but Seton...MacAllan...whoever he was now, held me back. He still had a pistol trained on his former body.

"Just for a few seconds more, Doctor, if you will," he said. "We need to ensure that the family will be able to maintain control; Moriarty's will is strong... but they are many."

And it did seem that he was right. The spasms *were* being brought under some degree of control. The body went still, the only sign of life being the eyeballs frantically moving under closed lids and the mouth working as if holding several simultaneous conversations.

"The boys will keep him busy," Seton said from his new body. "And I will keep him fed and watered. He will not be bothering society again – not for a *long* time."

Suddenly, just like that, I felt angry; enraged by the casual ease with which so many *souls* had been bartered. And I am afraid I took it out on Holmes.

"You knew," I said, rising to face him. "You knew all along that this would be the outcome."

Holmes, to his credit, looked glum.

"I knew there was a high chance of it, yes. As soon as I knew that Seton could duplicate Moriarty's strength of will and *inhabit* another body, then I knew."

"And you allowed it to happen. All those souls,

perished."

"Those are on Moriarty's conscience, not ours. It was he who forced those poor unfortunates to break the chain that bound them here, not I, and not Seton."

That made me turn my attention on the other man.

"And you – you are no better than Moriarty. What about the poor man whose body you now have? And him a kinsman of yours too. I..."

Seton's tears stopped me in my tracks.

"John is with his kin," he said, and motioned at the body on the ground. "Moriarty made him leave long before I ever got here. If it makes you feel any better, he has given me his blessing for what I have done."

"Blessing? I doubt there is anything of a *blessing* in any of this business."

Seton's eyes were red and he looked sadder than anyone I have ever seen.

"I agree with you on that point Doctor. But a discussion of the morality of my deeds will have to wait. I believe I will have a long time ahead of me to reflect on them." He turned to Holmes. "I know Lord Crawford is gone from my reach, but is Mycroft also keeping an eye on the one who survived?"

"Old Lord Menzies? Yes. And it would be fitting if his were to be the last actions in this matter, having been the one to bring us in to it in the first place. Tell him to send people to Dover. With luck and speed they should be there waiting for us."

Seton sat in a chair, rolled up his eyes, and was immediately *gone*. The body on the floor had also fallen quiet but on checking I saw that the eye movements were still rapid, and he was still mouthing words.

I looked up at Holmes.

"Maybe it would be for the best if we just shot the both of them?"

"Neither you nor I are capable of such a thing, Watson," he said. "Besides, shooting them would only release Moriarty from the prison where he resides."

"And I promise to keep him there for as long as I possibly can," Seton said, sitting up in the chair. "Mycroft has been informed. They will be waiting for us in Dover."

<<<—>>>

There is not much left to tell.

We spent a very disconcerting hour or so conversing with Seton in MacAllan's body while Moriarty, in Seton's body, lay mumbling on the floor.

"Having *moved* as it were, are you still immortal?" Holmes asked at one point.

Seton laughed. It seemed his humor had moved with him.

"I know not. I shall have to wait and see. Ask me again in fifty years or so."

When we pulled in to Dover Station there was a large police presence waiting. The train driver and two other accomplices were arrested. Holmes and I made sure the bullion was secure. After that we showed a team of shocked constables to the second Pullman carriage, and left them with the dead who lay there with their eyes filled with blood. When we returned to the rear carriage both Seton and his former body were gone, leaving no trace behind.

I never saw either of them again.

ENDS

About the Author

William Meikle is a Scottish writer with ten novels published in the genre press and over 200 short story credits in thirteen countries. He is the author of the ongoing Midnight Eye series among others, and his work appears in a number of professional anthologies. His ebook THE INVASION has been as high as #2 in the Kindle SF charts. He lives in a remote corner of Newfoundland with icebergs, whales and bald eagles for company. In the winters he gets warm vicariously through the lives of others in cyberspace, so please check him out at http://www.williammeikle.com